The Case of the Lost Mermaid

Rhiannon D. Elton

The Case of the Lost Mermaid © Rhiannon D. Elton 2021
The Wolflock Cases: Book 6
Second edition

ISBN: 978-0-6487636-5-9 (paperback)

First Edition published May 2017
Second Edition published April 2021

info@rhiannoneltonauthor.com

Cover compiled by Rhiannon D. Elton

This is a work of fiction. Names, characters, places, and incidents either are the products of the author's imagination or are used fictitiously. Any resemblance to actual persons, living or dead, businesses, companies, events, or locales is entirely coincidental.

Cataloguing-in-Publication information for this title is listed with the National Library of Australia.

Published in Australia by Rhiannon D. Elton and Pelaia Adventures

Get More of the Magic & Mystery…

subscribe.rhiannoneltonauthor.com/more

If you want more clues, more magic and more mystery, let me know by going to the Case of the Lost Mermaid subscribe page.

You'll get clues, maps, sketches, behind the scenes stories, lore and much more! You'll also be the first to know when a new story is coming out so you can solve the mystery before your friends.

If you sign up with the magical link below, you'll also get a free downloadable map to follow Wolflock's journey to Mystentine University.

subscribe.rhiannoneltonauthor.com/more

Declaration of Intention

Merry meet,

The purpose of the books the author writes is to give representation to as many peoples, creatures and landscapes as they can. Although written from the perspective of a Caucasian teenage boy, the author hopes to offer a light into the harmony of different cultures and creeds of people. The author's aim is to promote harmony, understanding and compassion in all areas, while also inspiring readers to stand up against injustice and be critical thinkers in life.

While the author does their best to research, interview and highlight the best parts of people, they are only human and can make mistakes. The author asks you gently educate them by sending them an email in order to discuss anything that may have caused harm to a group of people unintentionally.

The author believes that the cure for ignorance is education, but please approach the topic cordially in order to avoid any knee-jerk cognitive dissonance.

Finally, the viewpoints displayed in the books comes from a particular character and is not necessarily that of the author's. The author seeks to display flaws, growth and human nature on many levels, and hopes that you will analyse the character of the protagonist without adopting any negative behaviours from them.

Merry part, and merry meet again.

Rhiannon Op Elton

Mystentine University
Mystentine City
Vaggafel Forest
Hivrföa Forest
Creast
Iırid
Hatfjorn Lake
Wourst
Shorsh
Dragon's Spine Mountain Range
Lordr Pass
Krieger Zwerg Keep
Lelughwin Forest
Forestria
Zulber River
Woods of Dunkelheit
Plugh
0   100
Scale in Miles
Seebruecke Dock
Woods of Veil
(c) 2018 Rhiannon D. Elton

CHAPTER 1
The Daughters of the Sea

Wolflock pinched his chin, looking at the open barrel before him with a hint of a smirk.

"I see. This is a mystery indeed," he nodded, leaning down to look closer at the dried oats.

"Now, yeh hear me, Wolflock." Grogen put his hands on his hips and leaned down as well. "I know we had barrels o' dried dates, apples, peas, and flour. Even the crate with vinegar bottles, too! I saw 'em yesterday. And I can't find the suet, either! Me muffins are gonna be so bland."

"And that would be a travesty." Wolflock subtly covered his mouth with his hand as he heard a wheezy snicker from the back corner. "Tell me, Grogen. Has anyone tampered with your desserts before?"

"Not tha' I can remember. Only thievin' em, but I wouldn' call tha' tamperin'."

"I see. And who has been permitted access to the hull within the last day?"

"Just tha normal crew, I s'pose."

"Hmmm... And are you certain *every* barrel is filled with oats now?"

"Pretty certain."

"What about that barrel over there?" Wolflock pointed a thin finger at a large barrel at the back of the hull.

"Huh? Why that one?"

"It's recently been dragged from the oats section. You can tell by the dust along the floor. It's not the normal grey dust, but, rather, a fine cream colour."

"Yeh right." Grogen followed the trail to the barrel that was as big as him.

"I'd say what you're after may very well be in there." Wolflock glanced at the giggling box a few steps away as Grogen lifted the barrel lid and looked in.

"I can't see nothin'."

"It's a bit dark in here. Can you feel anything at the bottom?"

The large crewman grunted as he reached in, his feet lifting off the ground as he tried to touch the bottom.

"I can't feel nothing, Wolflock. It's empty."

"That can't be correct. Keep looking. I'll get a lantern for you." Wolflock lied as he crossed his arms and chuckled, watching Grogen's feet flailing out the top of the container.

One of the sides fell off the box the giggling was coming from and Mothy fell out of it, clutching his stomach as he guffawed. Wolflock burst out with laughter and rushed to seal the box back up again, leaving a little crack for Mothy to continue watching.

"Wha' was tha'?" Grogen's voice came muffled from the barrel.

"Nothing! I just tripped. I'll be back with a lantern presently." Wolflock composed himself as best he could.

"Don' worry. I found it."

The barrel wobbled on its rim as Grogen hoisted himself back out, triumphantly holding a tiny wooden fish with an opal for one eye.

"Wha' in Houl's name...?"

Wolflock gasped, covering his mouth to hide his

smile. "Oh. It all makes sense. I knew it."

"Knew what?"

"It's the," Wolflock dropped his voice to a whisper and beckoned Grogen closer, "pirate reedbits."

Grogen's brown eyes went wide at the mention of the corrupted guardians of Houl's river. The word 'pirate' was rarely spoken on the ship because the crew believed it would attract them, even though there hadn't been any along the river in hundreds of years.

"What do yeh mean, lad?"

The hushed tremor in the crewman's voice made it hard to keep a straight face. "Slavidus told me a few days ago about the tale of the pirate reedbits. Reedbits that renounced Houl and were punished to never be able to touch the river bottom again, but also to never leave the river, either. They cause all kinds of mayhem. Stealing food and turning the rest to oats to punish Houl's followers was their modus operandi. It looks like they're ready to parlay with us, though."

"How do you know that?"

"The fish. When they leave the sign of the fish, they're ready to discuss terms. They do the same thing with Houl when the river freezes over. They finally get a chance to rest in Winter when they are frozen in the ice."

"Well... we have the fish. How do we parlay with

'em?"

"Slavidus said that you have to look for the shadow of a reedbit and follow it without looking at it directly. Then they'll state their claims and if it's unreasonable you say, '*fiddle dee fiddle dit, that just won't work, nasty reedbit.*"

"And?" Grogen twisted his hands around the small wooden fish.

"You get three tries. The third one you have to agree to, or else they'll sink the ship or eat a passenger."

"What!?" Grogen gasped. "That can't be right!"

"I don't make the rules. I just repeat them."

"And break them." Mothy whispered loudly from the box.

Wolflock coughed and kicked his heel on the edge of the box to muffle the sound. Grogen frowned and looked around them for the source of the noise. Suddenly, Wolflock pointed behind Stra's storage area. "What's that?"

"Huh?"

"I just saw it! The reedbit shadow!"

Grogen raced over and Wolflock pointed further along. "There! Did you see it?"

"I can't see nothin', lad!" the burly sailor growled.

"Over there! Quick!"

"Ain't be 'sposed ta not be lookin' at it?" he grumbled as he squeezed between trunks further up.

"I keep seeing it out of the corner of my eyes."

"Your round eyes," Mothy whispered again.

Wolflock made Grogen chase the imaginary shadow all about the hull until finally he shut the box with a loud snap.

"I think we've got it in here. Good job, Grogen."

"Well," he panted, leaning forward, and supporting his huge frame on his knees, "hopefully it has... some reasonable... demands..."

"I hope so too," Wolflock stifled a laughed. "Fiddle dee, fiddle dit, what do you want, reedbit?"

Mothy made chirping rabbit noises inside the box with the occasional bubbling sound.

"Fiddle dee fiddle dont, a chest of cheese is what we want."

Grogen, having regained his breath, stood up straight and looked about. "We don't have any cheese. Only oats."

"You'd best tell them then," Wolflock nodded solemnly.

"Ah... how's it go? Fiddle dee fiddle dit, that just won't work, nasty reedbit."

Mothy tapped on the box like a rabbit thumping

the ground, which perfectly masked Wolflock stifled laugh.

"Fiddle dee fiddle doth. We want a ream of golden cloth."

Grogen scratched his brown beard, thinking for a long moment. "Do yeh reckon Haatji would give up some o' hers?"

"Oh, she doesn't have any to spare. It's all made into clothes already. She had to leave any reams for mending back in Uluken."

Grogen thumped the box with his hairy paw, "Ship rats!" he cursed. "Fiddle dee fiddle dit, that just won't work, nasty reedbit."

Mothy thumped the box again in rabbit like fashion and laughed in character. "Whoo, whoo, whoo! Fiddle dee fiddle die."

Grogen swallowed nervously as the word 'die' was mentioned.

"All I want is your best meringue pie."

The hull was silent as Grogen looked about. "Is... is it jokin'?"

Wolflock shrugged and made a face. Mothy hadn't told him he was going to ask for desserts.

"Is what joking? Grogen what are you doing in the hull? You're meant to be resting for your watch tonight."

Wolflock and Grogen looked up to the hull stairs and watched the first mate Slavidus descend with narrowed eyes. It was Wolflock's turn to gulp. He wasn't meant to be in the hull.

"Tha…" Grogen's eyes darted back and forth before he whispered, "… pirate reedbit, sir."

Slavidus frowned. "The what?"

"It's asking for me meringue pie, sir. Don't you worry though. I'll make it good and proper and then no crew or company'll be stolen."

Wolflock was glad the hull was so dark because the mix of nerves from being found by Slavidus and holding back his hysterical laughter made his face flush red hot.

"You take care of that. What are you doing here, Mr Felen?"

Before Wolflock could make up an excuse Grogen interrupted, "But we don' have no more eggs! It's all oats, sir!"

Slavidus' frown deepened. "What?"

"Oh wait!" Wolflock dashed forward and seized the lid of one of the oats crates, burying his arm elbow deep inside it. "Who'd have guessed! Eggs! Just under an inch or so of oats. Ha. So peculiar."

He tried to shake his head and pretend to be as perplexed as Grogen was, but Slavidus' stare sliced right through him.

"Oh! Maybe jus' the promise of my best was good enough to fix it? I'll get right onto it." He lifted the crate of eggs, but Slavidus put his hand on it.

"I'll get someone to help clear those oats out for you, Grogen. You get back to your normal duties."

"Yessir. Thanks for yeh help, lad."

Wolflock pushed his black hair behind his ear and nodded sheepishly, eyeing the hull stairs. The noise of Grogen's footsteps faded away before Slavidus turned and looked around the hull.

"Where's the other one?"

The teen shrugged, unable to stop his eyes flicking to the box, "Who?"

Slavidus rolled his grey eyes and kicked the box, making the side fall with a defeated thump. Mothy tucked himself tighter into the box.

"Out here now, Mothy."

"I'm the envoy for the pirate reedbits and I demand meringue for peace on this vessel," Mothy chirped into his knees, refusing to look up.

"Never seen a blond reedbit before, pirate or no. Out. Now. I won't ask again."

"I'm the-"

"Out!"

Mothy scrambled out and stood at attention next to Wolflock, mimicking his posture with a wry grin.

"You'll both take every single barrel upstairs, take out every single dried oat and put it in its proper place. Then you'll receive your punishment."

"What? But you don't have any proof it was us! We could have just found it and made fun of it." Wolflock snapped.

"Yeah! It could have been the pirate reedbits."

Slavidus' stony expression faced them both with the utmost fed up expression. He took a slow breath and came nose to nose with Wolflock. "Reedbits aren't smart enough or irritating enough to cause the same havoc on the ship as you."

Wolflock looked sideways at Slavidus. "I'm not sure if accepting that compliment would implicate me further."

"Both of you. Barrels. Upstairs. Now."

Moaning and grumbling, Wolflock hauled the barrels of food stores up into the crew quarters, then the passenger cabin hallway. Mothy, as always, acted like even their punishments were a fun adventure, making a worker's song out of the thump and roll. Crate by crate, barrel by barrel, Wolflock could have sworn they got heavier with each one.

Slavidus oversaw each and every one, making sure that everything was collected and not a single oat was spilled. Wolflock glared at his smug face whenever he trudged passed. Every now and then, the first mate would chuckle and shake his head. Finally, they tried to move a barrel onto the top deck, only to be accosted by a wild sheet flapping in the wind. As it buffeted around them, the pair nearly dropped the barrel. Unlike the normal clear deck with shapely sails and still masts, the current deck was shrouded in sheets and laundry, looking more like giant mismatched cobwebs.

"I suppose you'll have to take down your climbing sheets. The extra rigging is definitely in the way."

Wolflock rolled his eyes, not looking forward to having to climb up through the masts to take down their morning's entertainment. It had been a fun idea at the time, trying to build hammocks and rope bridges out of the laundry they'd been made to hang out for losing the half barrel they'd been riding in last night. The only reason they'd had the half barrel was because they'd had to do the dishes in it as punishment for changing some of the recipes in the ship's cookbook to riddles only they knew the answer to.

Wolflock didn't know why that had been an issue in the first place, as he thought it was an important mental exercise. It would also keep the recipes secret from thieves. The crew weren't sure why Wolflock wanted to keep the recipes secret, but he explained it was a Plugh thing.

Mothy decided that the best way to unravel their poorly tied laundry was to swing off them until they wriggled loose, attempting to do a roll before he hit the deck. The passengers milling around in the dappled sunshine thought this was the best entertainment they'd had all day. Wolflock refused to allow others to enjoy his punishment.

"You know," Slavidus watched them thoughtfully as the last sheet was pulled free, "I think I see a pattern to the problem you've both been having. Get to folding now."

"Pulling them down was all you asked us to do!" whined Wolflock.

"What pattern?" Mothy asked as he began shaking the sheet at Wolflock to make him grab the other end of it and help him fold.

"Neither of you can tie a decent knot. All your mischief gets you into trouble because you can't tie knots. Lost skis, lost barrels, yanking the sails in the wrong direction, your parasailing fiasco-"

The boys looked at each other and snickered.

"Knots. That's your issue. Anyway, once the laundry is done, bring the barrels up here and start putting all the oats back into their proper containers. I need a cuppa before changeover."

Slavidus turned away, his salt and pepper ponytail catching in the wind like an eel as he stretched and made his way to the dining hall.

The boys finished bringing the barrels onboard after another hour and chatted while they scooped the oats back into their original barrel. Their prank had been to put a half foot of oats on top of every food store in the hull and see how many crewmates they could fool until they got caught. They hadn't thought they would get caught.

Scoop by scoop, they cleaned out the dried oats in the brittle warmth of the sun as it spent a few lazy hours heating the little sea. Wolflock soon grew bored from the mundane task at hand, and his eyes began wandering along the glittering blue water that met the horizon.

It had been a week since they had left the Dragon's Spine pass; the gigantic mountains which had been on either side of them, dusted with snow at their peaks, while thick lichen and stubby grass clung to the boulders at their feet. One of the stories the crew told regularly was how the mountains were the knees of sleeping giants and the boulders were their toes. The children on board had been frightened by the story, as it finished with, "if you are too loud in the pass, you'll wake them up", at which point Wolflock and Mothy, who had been hiding in the crow's nest, had let out deep shouts meant to sound like giants and caused a few rocks to tumble into the water with the echoes.

They'd been banned from hiding in the crow's nest during the day for that very reason.

Wolflock sighed as he looked out at the watery nothingness. That was boring now, too. He was starting to miss the forest banks teeming with wildlife, and the ancient shapes of the mountains through the pass.

The day rolled on with the languid waves and Wolflock thumped his fist on the last barrel lid to close it, leaving an off-white coloured print from the dust on his hands. He arched his back and stretched out, relieved that the task was finally done. Mothy had begun rolling the barrels, one by one, back down into the hull, foreseeing that Slavidus would ask them to do it anyway. He felt tired just watching Mothy painstakingly steady the barrels with his thin frame as he lowered them, step by step, back down.

Wolflock stared for as long as it took Mothy to get one barrel down the stairs, his blue eyes darting back and forth. There had to be an easier way. When Mothy came back up, wiping the sweat from his brow, Wolflock stopped him before he rolled another barrel to the stairs.

"Give me two moments. Stand here. Yes. That's it. Now hold the barrel in place. Rope. We need rope."

He dashed around the deck, grabbing a mop, a bucket and sixty feet of rope attached nearby. As Mothy watched on in amazement, Wolflock fashioned a pulley system around the barrel.

"There! That should make things easier!" He stood back, proudly admiring his handiwork. "Just don't let the rope reach its end, otherwise the whole thing will unravel. And don't let the mop slide off the railing here."

"Why is that?" Mothy asked, testing the new pulley.

"Well, it might crash onto someone at the bottom of the stairs. I thought that was obvious, Mothy. Now, get back to it. Scooping oats for hours has given me a new idea for how we can fasten the tables and chairs of the dining hall to the ceiling for a laugh."

He left Mothy to his new toy while he strolled around the deck, hoping for any interesting thing to come into view. Apparently, that was only Fuhji proceeding to run past him to vomit over the side of the ship.

"By Houl..." she groaned, wiping her mouth with

a wet cloth, "these waters are turning my stomach inside out..."

"It's not Houl you have to pray to, Miss." Captain Blutro came down from his duties at the helm while Canhop relieved him for the changeover. "We're in Aygir and Hatfjorn's domain now."

The children on board, who normally played games on the open deck, knew that when Captain Blutro mentioned one of the gods of the region or any distinct name with a particular tone of voice, that he was about to tell a story. Like the call of the pied piper, their ears pricked up and Gege, Didi, and Tanni made their way over, their big eyes glittering with anticipation.

Happy to have an enthusiastic audience, Captain Blutro cleared the space around the centre mast.

"Once upon a time there was no sea here-"

"I thought it was a lake," Wolflock heckled from the cabin stairs.

"It's attached to the ocean via the Western outlet, now, hush, lad. The Hatfjorn Sea didn't-"

"Isn't it the 'Silver' Lake, though?" he shouted out again, laughing.

"Oh, you're asking for it, lad." Captain Blutro waved his finger in warning. "It's a sea, no matter what the maps from the East landers made popular, and it's called

Hatfjorn, no matter what the Southerners get lazy with. Not everything attached to the history of the King's bloodline is called 'silver'. Now! As I was saying," he eyed Wolflock suspiciously, but Wolflock gave him a shrug to concede, "there was a time when the sea was completely ice. The old god Aygir didn't like anything that scurried or moved or grew, so he froze the path so nothing could live in his territory. One day, a maiden of fire skated across his surface, immune to his frost and a master of the elements. She was said to be made of flames and she danced eternally. It was her heat that melted Aygir's frozen heart. And what do you think her name was?"

The children stayed silent and avoided his gaze.

"Hatfjorn," came a laugh from Wolflock's side. Dlumi, the businesswoman from Corsh, was a native to Shiriling, so of course she'd know the tale. "I haven't heard this one since I was a *pozo.*"

"Dlumi gets an extra dessert tonight," chuckled the Captain.

"Pozo?" Wolflock asked. He had never heard the word before and it didn't sound like any other word he could relate it to.

"Sorry. Child. The closer we get to home the more I slip into Shirth."

"Did you know Shirth is one of the influences for

Nördlicherwald? As well as... never mind."

Dlumi wasn't listening. The Captain was speaking about how Aygir melted for his lady and, as she matured, she grew heavy and sank beneath him to become the lava vents that keep the centre of the sea unfrozen during Winter. The edges all froze as Winter demanded the world go to sleep.

"... Together, Hatfjorn and Aygir had a thousand sons. So many, they forgot the names of them. But they only had nine daughters, who they treasured above all else. The first three were Bloughadda, the Shirth name for the sunset light on the crest of the wave; Bylgia, whose name means the billowing sound of waves; and Drofn, who is the wave that breaks on the shore. To the first three daughters, the first creature to give its blessings was always the octopus. For this, the octopuses in Hatfjorn were welcomed into the society of mermaids for their intelligence and kindness."

"What's an octopus?" Tinni asked in awe.

"It's a squishy creature with a head bigger than yours and eight long legs. They are very smart, and, sometimes if you're lucky, you'll see one come to the surface to chase a fish. But that is exceedingly rare indeed," Captain Blutro explained, wiggling his fingers in an octopus interpretation. "The next three daughters were Duufa, the thud of a wave; Hefring, the rise of the water; and Hronn, the rumble and foam of a crashing wave. It was the hammerhead sharks who blessed them. In return, Aygir gave them agility so they may always catch their prey and never go hungry."

"There's a significant amount of words for 'wave' in Shirth. Any reason why?" Wolflock interjected.

Dlumi pouted her lips as she thought. "I live inland, so, for us, that's all poetry stuff. But I suppose it's some kind of a safety or knowledge thing, because the water can be dangerous. For Corshfolk, we have fifteen different words for snow. Brown snow, slush, powder, uh... It gets tricky to translate them. But each one helps us know where is safe, where to tread, and where to find the things we want."

"That may well be very true for sailors having nine words for the parts and motions of a wave." Wolflock nodded slowly as he listened back into the story.

"And the final three daughters were Kolga, the wave of ice; Himiglaeven, the light reflected off the sea; and Unn, the deep rolling wave that lifts and drops the ship. The dolphins came to the births and blessings of these three daughters, so Hatfjorn gave them the gift of the currents that weave like reeds through the entire sea. She knew dolphins liked to play as much as her, so she used her hot breath to blow the currents back and forth with the breath of the sea.

"Aygir warmed for his wife and daughters, but he still had a heart of ice, and so, fragile, and susceptible to heat, he knew he had to protect his heart. He had to make a place to keep it safe. Aygir drew up all his magic and created a great castle in the heart of the sea. That castle was called Sinalta, where only his children could live. To make sure all his children were safe, he made them keep their hearts in the castle, too. They may give them away, but they may never be stolen."

"What happens if they give their heart away?" Tinni asked.

"It is said that anyone who holds the heart of one of Aygir and Hatfjorn's children need never fear drowning. For the rest of us, we just hope the dolphins float us to the shore before we freeze." Captain Blutro let out a hearty laugh, but the children quivered at the mention of freezing and drowning. "We might just see some dolphins today! Quick! Go look."

"Again! Again!" Dlumi clapped as the children ran to the taffrail. Captain Blutro gave her a bow, swirling his hands as he dipped forward. "Ah. It makes me homesick. I'll be glad to go back."

"Speak for yourself. If I ever have to go back to

Plugh, it will be too soon."

"Lucky for you then." Wolflock jumped as Slavidus gripped his shoulder, steering Mothy up beside him. "I have plenty of work for you to do on board."

"But didn't we just do our..." Mothy thought for the word.

"Recompense," Wolflock offered.

"Aye! Recompense for the oats crime," he nodded, satisfied with the word. Wolflock gave him a wide-eyed stare. They'd agreed to continue to pretend they were innocent of the matter. Mothy caught his stare and shook his hands. "Which we didn't do in the first place!"

"This is less a punishment and more a lesson. Trust me. You boys need it. Grogen!" he shouted across the way to the burly crewman talking at Hognut, who smoked his pipe in silence. "Help these two learn how to tie a real knot. When you're satisfied they won't be able to lose anymore Silver Ice Hair property, they can go about their normal fun."

Grogen's face twisted into an unconvinced grimace.

"What? You don't think they can learn a good tie down?"

"It's not tha', sir. It's more me worry 'bout what'll

they do when they do learn."

Slavidus chuckled darkly and patted Grogen's shoulder. "If we find any knots tied in abnormal places or manners, we'll know who to make unravel the mess. Besides, Captain's suggestion will keep them safe in the long run."

"The Captain asked you to teach us how to tie ropes?" Wolflock raised his eyebrow.

"Oh, aye. After I suggested it, he was adamant. We only have a week left with most of you, so I can't imagine you'll get up to too much trouble. Not with the crew on alert for it all."

Mothy and Wolflock smirked at one another as the reluctant Grogen hauled several lengths of rope, twine, and cord before them. "You pair untangle that. I'll show yeh the basics. If yeh any good, I'll show yeh the not so basics."

The afternoon went much faster as Wolflock and Mothy learned the overhand knot, the sailor's knot, square knots, lark's head, and figure eight knots. They started to play a game where Grogen would call out a scenario as if the deck were a dance hall, and make the boys run to the right location and tie the correct knot to imaginary stage lights, props, and platforms. They got through eel knots, killick hitches, and pats paw binds, getting faster with the game and the competition.

Wolflock eventually learned all forty knots Grogen set out for them and could tie them right from his memory without prompting, proclaiming their purpose with smug satisfaction. Mothy was bright enough to learn twenty of the less complicated ones, but they were sufficient nonetheless.

As the apricot horizon melded into the dusty blue sky, a blanket of thick black clouds rolled over the ship, sealing in what little warmth the sun had given them through the day.

Wolflock and Mothy were only distracted by their new hobby when Matroos, one of the crewmen from Syongdelen, stumbled over Tinni as she ran to the other side of the ship. She had run and slipped, causing him to drop the crate of instruments he'd been carrying back down into the crew quarters as he reflexively saved her from hurting herself.

"Be more careful, little one," he sighed in a voice so deep it commanded silence from even the seabirds flying overhead.

"Is she injured, Matroos?" Grogen frowned, leaping to his feet at the commotion.

"No, mate. Are you hurt, little miss?" He turned her this way and that, making her giggle and cling to his midnight black hand with her tawny red ones. "I think she's all well."

Wolflock wasn't focused on the pair, though. His piercing blue eyes were locked on one of the instruments that had fallen out of the box.

"Is that a violin?" he breathed.

Matroos blinked at him. "Ya. Do you play?"

Mothy moved forward to help pick up the tambourines and percussion mallets.

"Does a horse run? Of course, I play."

The crewman shrugged. "If you can tune it, you can play it. No one onboard can play. If you play badly, though, Cap'in will string you up. Was his old ma's."

Wolflock snatched up the instrument like a starving cretin and plucked at the strings. They were loose and twanged with a sagging tone.

"Huh. I think this might take a while."

"It's your turn to sit with Parihaan," Mothy said as he put the loose instruments back in Matroos's box. "Maybe tune it and have a practice there? I'll find the bodhrán I saw earlier, and we can make a few songs. Nü has a pretty instrument in her case. She could join us when Geagle takes his watch."

Wolflock barely heard a word Mothy said. He picked up the rickety old case and bow and made his way downstairs without a word. The feel of the sleek, curved wood under his fingers, the minute roughness of the G and D strings, the elegant swirl of the scroll... it made his heart ache. He hadn't realised how much he missed playing until his eyes prickled. Just holding the untuned violin made his whole being yearn for it.

He dismissed Nü with their usual short sentences and took up his seat next to the unconscious Parihaan, plucking at the strings while he twisted the pegs in infinitesimal increments. With each note closer to the pure one, he felt the instrument become as rejuvenated as he was by its sound.

Finally tuned, he practiced his scales and was taken back to his only happy moments at home, and some of the few times his father smiled at him. Remembering a few shorter songs and the favourite bars of his most played pieces, Wolflock put on a plucky, disjointed concert for Parihaan.

He rested his hand down on the bow.

Now for a real try. He grinned, drawing up the bow and beginning a slow and easy tune. The sound resonated through the cabin and lifted him like wind under wings. He stood up and turned about the room, playing more jovially.

Then, a purple and orange flash caught his eye and

he stopped, staring at the open door.

"We're so sorry," one of the Quaretz twins giggled, only a manicured hand and glittering violet eye peeping from the doorframe. "We didn't want you to stop playing."

Wolflock smiled, relaxing his shoulders and bringing the bow up to the strings. He played a soft tune as he crept to the door. The twins, Bleen and Faleen, were peeking in as he burst through the door, playing with more vigour and pep than he had in private.

They squealed and applauded as he took a bow.

"You have such a natural talent!" Bleen giggled and clapped, her lush purple hair swimming around her face in thick locks.

"Yes. You are very good," Faleen nodded.

Standing either side of Parihaan's door, the Quaretz twins were a visual cacophony. Faleen dressed in vibrant layers of orange, yellow and red, with hair shorn short and dyed an unnatural tangerine colour. Her sister, Bleen, dressed in deep shades of blue and purple, which seemed to be their natural hair colour as Wolflock noted Faleen's dark regrowth.

"I was classically trained for eleven years in piano, Grothien horn, and violin," he said as he puffed out his chest.

"You have a calling for music. That is clear." Faleen exhaled, her tone implying he should have already been aware of this.

He felt confused about her response. Over the past week, he had engaged in many conversations with the Quaretz twins. They had travelled far and wide telling fortunes, and were a wealth of knowledge from different lands. Bleen always showed the utmost enthusiasm for their talks, picking fluff and dust from his clothes, straightening his hair, and showing him their story-rich trinkets. Faleen acted in a similar way to her sister, but then, seemingly at random, would stand tall, look down her nose at him and give short, sharp responses, as if he'd offended her. The contrast between their attitudes and appearances became greater each time he interacted with them. What perplexed Wolflock, though, was how he had obtained such differing opinions from both when they had seen him act and speak to everyone in a similar fashion.

"You have to play for everyone on the deck," Bleen tittered, linking arms with him as she drew him to the stairs.

"Unfortunately," he pulled his arm free, "I am on duty to keep Miss Nebralt company in case she wakes. You'll have to give me leave until Geagle comes to replace me."

Bleen pouted and Faleen's sharp, dark eyebrow raised.

"Very well. But we'll miss you at dinner," simpered the purple twin, plucking an oat from his sleeve with her long purple nails.

Faleen said nothing, walking ahead of her sister.

Normally, Wolflock only had to ask Mothy what he had done or said to offend someone, but even he didn't know why Faleen was amicable some days and cold the next. Wolflock shrugged and moved back into Parihaan's room, playing lightly for her. As he repeated the same few songs over and over, he wished for some sheet music. He knew the Captain had some in his quarters, but he wouldn't leave Parihaan alone.

His shift passed and he put down the violin, hearing splashing outside the ship. It was odd to him because it didn't follow the natural rhythm of the waves he'd been playing to. Haatji came to relieve him after dinner, saying that Geagle was called on to deck duties. Wolflock felt full from the music he'd enjoyed and didn't want to cloud his head with the rich stew Matroos had made up. The Syongdelen spices were powerful and earthy, often leaving him feeling exhausted.

Instead, he leaned on the railing of the starboard

side of the deck and watched the black waters glinting in the light of the crescent moon.

Music helped him think. It always had. It helped him express himself when he couldn't find the words. It gave him solace and relief from the tension of life at Plugh. Wolflock played a silky-smooth tune to the water, lost in thought. He took time to think about all the mental webs he'd woven throughout his time on the ship.

Finding the Captain's pet snuffle, discovering the truth about his best friend's past, locating the source of the sickness that plagued the ship, solving the smuggling case the Captain had set for him, and, finally, discovering how Parihaan had fallen down the stairs. Amongst all his neatly laid webs, particular strands stood out to him. Reflecting off his music like the moon off the water. Or the shine of light off a strangely shaped knife.

His notes quickened.

The person who had tried to kill Parihaan still hadn't been discovered. He remembered them sneaking into her room. Raising their blade. If he hadn't called out, she would have been murdered.

Then there was the third shoeprint in the hull. Someone had gone down there, seen Parihaan's body and left without raising the alarm.

He still had in his possession the letter he found

when he came back to consciousness, addressed from the mysterious 'A'. There was also the strange purple sea slug and the handkerchief with the peculiar powder.

He wondered what other clues had evaded him due to his ignorance. As he played and the threads grew brighter in his mind, he felt deep in his gut a gratitude for the luck of having this instrument placed in his hands. The mysterious hooded figure with the knife wouldn't be able to evade him when he felt so clear of thought.

As his thoughts played through his head like the song on his strings, a deep heartbeat rhythm rumbled through them. Wolflock opened his eyes to see Mothy approaching him, beating a bodhrán drum, holding it at the cross with his left hand and tapping it with the matching tipper.

"Merry meet, my friend," Wolflock beamed.

"Merry meet. You were so deep in thought I didn't want to disturb you."

"Not at all. It has been too long since I've played an instrument with finesse. It brings me back to a... clearer version of myself."

"That's dangerous," Mothy chuckled and beat the drum at an even pace.

"Aye. Speaking of danger, what do you think we'll get up to at Mystentine?"

"Not sure. I like to play things by ear when it comes to mischief. I want to watch the sun rise and set from their highest tower. And I want to eat one of everything they have to serve."

"Noble ambitions. I want to study every class I deem relevant to my profession."

"I've never asked. What profession is that, exactly?"

"I... No one has ever asked me that before. I suppose you'd call it..." Wolflock fell silent. What was he to call himself?

"It's like a private detective, right?"

"But it's more than that. I don't want to just solve crime. I want to exercise my deductive reasoning."

"A puzzle solver?"

"I don't think that lends itself to the title I'm after. It gives a childish impression."

"What will you be doing? Let's nail it down from there."

"I envisioned people would see an advertisement on the local noticeboard, then send me a letter with a problem they have, a mystery. Something they can't solve. Something so perplexing that I'll have to use all my skills to put it together for them."

"Like a consulting detective?"

Wolflock and Mothy stopped playing their instruments for a moment and pondered his words before doubling over in fits of laughter.

"That's the most ridiculous title I've ever heard."

"I don't even know where it came from! It just popped out."

After a few moments, they wiped away their tears and waited for the residue of laughter to ebb before they spoke again.

"I think you might be on the right path, though. It's an investigation of some kind. Not as limited as detective work."

"Like... an investigator who appraises the case first. Because if it isn't going to help anyone and is just a flight of fancy, I can't see you taking it."

"Less about helping people and more about how interesting it is. Hmm... Appraising Investigator..."

They sat on the words as Mothy drummed and Wolflock bowed.

"Appraising Investigator. Yes. Yes, I like it. I like it a lot!"

With each beat Wolflock felt the name awaken inside him, as if a spiritual heart had started to thump in his core. They played without words and Wolflock felt a deep-seated contentment with their solution.

Beside them, they heard a loud splash and clicking noises. They stopped playing and looked over the edge. Just dark water and the glimmer of light from Dlumi's room shining down.

With a shrug, they both began musing on again, but, after only a few seconds, another splash occurred. They stopped, looking at one another suspiciously, and leaned over to see the same inky waters from before. Wolflock drew out a long quavering note and then they saw it. A bright pink fish leaped from the water.

"Slavidus!" Mothy called as Wolflock continued to bow. "Slavidus! There's a pink fish!"

"Pink fish?" the first mate answered. "That ain't no fish lad! It's a dolphin."

"Dolphins ahoy!" Mothy sang out to the ship.

Faster than he'd ever seen the ship assemble, Wolflock played as the company crowded around him, waiting for the next appearance of their guest star. He played an upbeat tune and as if on cue, the dolphin leaped out of the water. Then a second, larger one followed, leaping out and turning to the side to look up at them with its big black eye.

For a good half hour, the company applauded the dolphins while the crew sang happy sea shanties. The curious creatures followed Wolflock's music for well over a mile. The loud humdrum on the top deck brought the Captain up to see what the commotion was.

He raised his eyebrows at seeing Wolflock play his great grandmother's violin, but his face proceeded to split into a smile when he looked over at the pink dolphins.

"This is a very good sign."

CHAPTER 2
Foretold Disaster

Wolflock slept with a smile on his face that night. Everyone had stayed up late, dancing to his and Mothy's music, and the Captain had brought out an old music book of folk songs and ship music. The cheeky tunes were simple, accompanied by rude and foolish lyrics. He was absolutely delighted that he had the chance to learn songs his father and Myna would have abhorred.

He dreamed of sitting in the middle of his iridescent mental web, plucking the strings to a beautiful tune, each one becoming clearer and singing their truth with each reverberating note. He could nearly see the face of the person with the knife. A new thread started to appear. Had the window to the kitchen been closed when the tuiti fruit had made everyone sick? If that were the case, the maramuti couldn't have put the river slugs in the pot. Had the person with the knife also tried to poison the Tuiti fruit stew?

Thinking about his least favourite fruit made him feel nauseous. The nausea woke him up and he was relieved it dissipated instantly as he sat up in the cool morning air. Wolflock could already hear passengers moving to breakfast and around the deck above him. He could also hear that odd splashing of the dolphins leaping out beside the ship to the light strumming of a guitar.

"It's a shame me old Warren doesn't bring 'em out like the drum and violin did last night." Grogen sighed; Wolflock heard him through his open window.

"Is that what you call your guitar?" Dlumi snickered.

"Me and old Warren go way back, young miss," Grogen snorted indignantly. "And, I'll have yeh know, this is the fifth guitar that ever made its way to Shiriling. Everyone who likes good music knows Warren brands are the best. Hardy, cheap, and the best sound for travellin'."

"So, the working man's guitar?"

They both laughed as Wolflock rolled out of bed and dragged on his black slacks. After he'd finished getting dressed, he heard Dlumi sigh. "It's a shame there isn't more opportunities for musicians in Shiriling."

"Whadaya talkin' bout? We get the best vocalists in the continent. Haven't yeh seen Madame Laesa Kennileiti Bjalla shatter the ice they build up for her concerts?"

"Who?"

"Madame- so uncultured yeh are."

Wolflock chuckled to himself as he finished eavesdropping and made his way to a late breakfast. For once, Mothy was up before him and having fifths while Nü made Parihaan's medicine. The sharp smell woke him up better than the green tea he'd grown fond of.

They heard the Captain's announcement bell from the helm, but, since Wolflock hadn't eaten yet and Mothy wanted sixths, they stayed in a bit longer, giving Nü the help she needed in between mouthfuls.

After breakfast, Wolflock made his way out onto the deck, enthusiastically playing silly little ditties on the violin while he looked for what the announcement might have been. A line of ten passengers stood before a small table where Faleen and Bleen were writing details down.

Ah. They're telling fortunes for everyone. I suspect

that is what they offered as payment for their journey.

Not one to wait in line, Wolflock sidled up to them at the table and plucked a jovial little tune for them. A hint of disappointment crossed his face when not even Bleen giggled at his antics.

"I'll take whatever last timeslot is remaining."

Faleen turned her head like a menacing chicken and peered side eyed at him with a cold smile. "That's not how this works, Mr Felen. You'll have to wait your turn like everyone else."

"Oh, fret not, Faleen. I'll wait if I must. I just wanted to show my support for you performing your payment to the ship and make sure I had an opportunity to experience your expertise."

"Indeed. Well-"

"Oh, don't worry, Wolflock," Bleen stretched her fingers and jotted down his name at the top of the list. We have a special spot for you. Don't you recall, sister? We were going to speak to him very first."

"Ah. Yes. That's right. The moon will be in the phoenix junction by dinner and it's best to get the more..." She stopped and looked Wolflock up and down with her violet eyes. He saw she had a bright orange streak in the right-hand corner of her right eye. "Well. No matter. Bleen is correct. We had intended to speak with you first."

"I look forward to it. Merry part, ladies."

"And merry meet again," Bleen sang as Froderyk stepped up to the table.

Pleased he didn't have to wait in line, Wolflock made his way to the starboard side of the ship to compose a new song for the dolphins to dance to. Mothy joined him soon after with the bodhrán and they spent a merry morning playing together. Captain Blutro commented that if music were the way to keep them out of trouble, he would have made a passenger ensemble weeks ago.

Just after lunch, Geagle approached them, looking pale. "Good afternoon Mr Wolflock, sir. Ms and Ms Quaretz have requested your presence in their cabin. And Mr Mothy, Miss Nü wants you to take my shift. There's rough waters coming up and I'm needed on deck for longer hours than I can afford."

"Aye, aye, Mr Geagle," Mothy saluted. Geagle departed and Wolflock put the violin in the case. "Good luck. Make sure you take notes and tell me everything they tell you. I'm just as excited for what they say to you as they'll say to me tomorrow."

"Tomorrow? Aren't they starting everyone's readings now?"

"No. I think everyone but you are booked in for

tomorrow and the next day."

"Hmm. They must have a very special reading for me indeed."

"What do you think they're going to say?"

"I'm not sure. I've never had a fortune reading before. I'm hoping they'll help me know what classes to take at Mystentine and if there are particularly clever people I should look out for. Some forewarning on how I should look at describing and structuring my profession would also be welcome."

"As the friend and nephew of the metaphysically inclined, the term you're looking for is *career*."

Wolflock rolled his eyes with a grin. "Aren't you eloquent today?"

"What can I say? Your elevated vocabulary heightens mine when I am in your presence."

"And I further become immune to your flattery."

"Go on. Stop yammering with me and get to your future!"

Wolflock made his ways downstairs and, in his excitement, arrived at the twin's cabin door with the violin case still in hand. He raised his hand to rap on their grey door, but it opened before he could knock. Faleen, in her autumnal shades, stood before him with a condescending smile he chose to ignore.

"I'm so glad you came on time."

"Wolflock! Come in, come in. We're so happy. This is such an important reading for you. We've been feeling it come through for weeks now. The power of this waxing crescent moon is just enough to help give our abilities a little boost and give you the answers we know you need."

Bleen pushed passed her sister and drew him into their cabin, her hands soft, yet firm with her grasp. The thick smell of incense and essential oils flooded his sinuses, making it hard to take a deep breath. Scarves, ribbons, and tapestries with all manner of sigils and wards were strewn across the walls and ceiling, making the room snuggly warm, but also oppressive. A small table was set in the middle of the room between two single beds, and cushions were laid out for seats around it. A deep purple satin tablecloth shimmered in the glittering lantern light. The fairy dust lanterns in their room were covered with red and blue clothes, adding a soft purple hue to the grey wood in the room.

"Please, take a seat. Would you like some tea?"

"What kind is it?" Wolflock asked, sniffing the air, and noting unfavourable hints of fruitiness.

"It's the tea we're serving you." Faleen smiled, pressing the cup into his hands.

As he sipped it to be polite, he tasted the sickly sweet, dried fruit and acidic sulphur preservatives he knew would give him a headache later. He much preferred Nü's light but bitter green tea. Bleen put her hands on Wolflock's shoulders and pushed him down on a particular cushion. He folded his legs and looked around at the wards and tapestries. He also took note of a beautiful parcel with a large ornate card. He couldn't make out what it said in its entirety, but it ended with *"...and Astraxis can make this into the incense of your dreams. Love Gilmere."*

"Gifts from our travels along the border of Uluken and Xiayah. Most from some form of nobility, and those three with gold embroidery from her majesty, Queen Sarabineesa, herself." Faleen waved her hand lazily towards the draperies. "The tea is only of the highest quality from the Pryingelian cliffs, gifted for our palmistry from the duchess of Ta'akin point."

Wolflock had a small itch of doubt at that. *Why would royalty want to preserve tea with something as poor quality as sulphur?*

As if she'd read his mind, Faleen's eyes snapped to him. "First. Things. First." She snipped. "You will turn off that analytical mind of yours. It is a detriment to everyone around you as much as it is yourself. There is no room for your logic that so cruelly tears apart the instinctual truth."

"I... Pardon?"

He heard Bleen slide close the door with a soft thud. "What my dear sister means is that in this room we are the leaders. We are the conduits for the analysis and information. The spirits that have been trying to speak through us for weeks will finally have a chance. You're not to try and glean minute details that could hinder the messages meant for you. Understand?"

Wolflock shrank back. How was he meant to just turn off who he was as if he was snuffing a candle?

"All we ask is that you have an open mind and don't disregard what we say because it doesn't initially agree with you. Understand?"

"Yes," he mumbled. Did they really think he was going to do something to offend them? They were his friends, were they not? Did they believe he would ruin the reading he had been looking forward to receiving?

As doubt shook through him, Faleen sighed with relief, "Ah. That is much better. Your aura has shrunk to a reasonable size. In such a small room, you must understand, Mr Felen, that your energy can be quite suffocating. Now we have room to also exist in this space."

Wolflock didn't know how to respond. Did everyone feel like that around him? Had he been fooled into thinking he had made friends? He felt completely tipped sideways by their words.

"Now, scatter and shuffle these cards so they go all topsy turvy. Think of a question or keep your mind blank. But just one question."

Wolflock stretched forward, squashing his stomach as he pushed the cards around on the table. As he moved their blackened floral designs around, he felt like someone had run salt water through his veins. They were older than him. They were more travelled than him. They had more experience. Surely, they were right?

"Now put them back together, then divide it into three. Now choose one pile," Bleen continued to smile at him, her chin resting on her fingertips and her face tilted to the side.

He chose the left-hand side.

Something felt off. He couldn't put his finger on it, but the room felt like cool wisps of air were trickling over his arms and he couldn't bring himself to smile. Faleen took up the deck and began laying out seven cards in a rough horseshoe shape before him.

She flipped the card furthest to his left.

"Ah, yes. Your past, of course, is the seven of

swords. I knew you would get many swords in this reading. There was a serious theft or fraudulent action against you. You were surrounded by lies, intrigue and the cunning of your opponents. Such a hard past. No wonder you are as you are."

"I don't know what you-"

"Uh, uh, uh!" Bleen tittered, waving her finger. "Just sit and listen. Don't analyse. Just absorb." She flipped the second card. "Oh, my dear. The Empress. This must be your mother. She is your present. Did she encourage your probing nature? Are you doing this all for her?"

Wolflock felt his heart palpitate and his throat tighten with a sharp, icy sensation.

"I-"

"Uh, uh, uh," Bleen teased, "For such a clever boy you have trouble with simple instructions, don't you? Silence now."

Faleen half smiled and flipped the third card, "Ah yes. The Fool. What you don't see. Fitting, isn't it?"

Wolflock kept his mouth closed.

"The Fool is the sign of a new journey. Of your naivety keeping you protected. But all naivety must be shed at some stage. You are going on a great journey and you will learn so many new things along the way. The

Fool is always a good sign for people starting out. His naivety about the world is what keeps him safe, but for you, your curiosity will be your downfall." Bleen hummed.

Wolflock nodded, his lips twisting into dissatisfaction at the Fool's reveal. He had a feeling these women knew what these mysterious cards meant for him specifically. It was as if they knew what he had drawn, and the cards were just the physical tool to show him what they'd already seen.

"Ah! The next one is the reversed Emperor. He is your greatest obstacle. A tyrant. A monster among men and often accepted by the unwitting. This is someone you never want to come into battle with. Mental or physical. They will annihilate you. This one has whispered echoes to us. He weaves a terrifying web of cruelty and malice, but you are not equipped to slay his slippery empire. Oh no. Your logic and deductions will never bring him down. This is the card I was hoping you would see." Faleen proceeded in a harsh whisper. "If you try, you will lose everything."

Bleen leaned forward and patted Wolflock's arm. He shied away. It wasn't comforting.

"This is what has been plaguing our conduit natures for weeks. This card tells us that you are your own worst enemy. You are your biggest obstacle. You're the only one who stands between you and greatness."

Wolflock frowned. He refrained from speaking though, letting them continue even though he burned with ever mounting questions.

Bleen flipped the fifth card with a quick motion. "This is how other people may influence your future. The reversed Chariot."

Faleen snorted.

"Pride and arrogance are how others see the situation. And... I'm sorry to say, but they aren't wrong."

Bleen's sympathetic tone seeped into Wolflock cracked emotional defences, but it felt stifling. Something was wrong with it. It was slimy and irritating. Her smile didn't reach her eyes and for the first time he saw a coldness to them. Violet orbs with that odd orange slice in the bottom left of the left eye. The mirror of her twin sister.

"This card signifies that the path you're on will be fraught with dangers and anyone who travels with you will suffer as well. And the next card-"

"The two of rods. Hmm... interesting," Faleen smiled smugly.

The twins looked at each other with the utmost satisfaction. Wolflock waited. They'd asked him to be quiet. After a long, grating silence, Faleen continued.

"This one shows your best path. This is what we suspected all along. You have a choice to travel peacefully. Throughout your journeys you'll have many partners come along with you, but the choice that lays before you is..."

Bleen flicked her purple nails to pick up the final card. "Ah yes. The Magician. He stands at a crossroads. He has a choice. You can guide your friends and family down a path that leads you to a fruitful, happy life of love and respect, or you can walk the dangerous and lethal road of darkness and despair."

The twins fell silent and stared expectantly at him.

"So..." he spoke with a tone laced with caution, pulling his knees up to his chest, "What is the good path and the bad path?"

"The good path has been clear to us ever since you picked up the violin on the ship. I knew there was a cloud around you, and music cleared it beautifully. The good path is your destiny to become a concert musician."

Wolflock jerked his head back. "What?"

"Oh yes. You are the best musician we have ever seen. Do not follow the exhilaration of the dark path before you. For that is the path we have seen you consistently choose." Faleen said in a low voice.

"What do you mean?"

"The path of investigating. The further you probe into other people's business, the more you pry and the more secrets you reveal, the more danger you put the people you love in. The more your family will be displeased with you. You put all their reputations in danger. You will remain poor and at the whims of the moment. There is no sustainability, no safety, no hope."

"Oh."

Wolflock felt his face drop and his eyes burn with tears. He'd just found the word he wanted to be with Mothy. He'd just felt that sensation of knowing his path, and it was being torn from him.

Bleen must have seen the change in his disposition because she made a move to reach out for him, but Faleen stared her down.

"Don't trouble yourself, Wolflock. You will travel far and wide as a musician. And, after you are well known, you will be able to pursue your investigating as a hobby. After that, you will have the funds and experience to do anything you want to, but you have to establish your real career first."

"What if this isn't correct?"

Faleen glared at him, "We are never wrong, and don't insult us by saying such things."

Wolflock recoiled at her snap. "But what if I just do it for a while and see how it goes?"

"Then you will have wasted precious years where you could be pursuing your real destiny," Bleen simpered.

"What if I perform and investigate? At the same time?"

"The irresistible darkness will continue to encapsulate you until it destroys you and those you love."

"But I-"

"Are you going to contest everything we say until you get your way?" Faleen rapped her long orange nails on the table in obvious irritation.

"Wolflock, Faleen and I have spent so much time with you over the past week, encouraging you, guiding you, and trying to help you in ways you may not have known you needed. Are you really going to hurt us by wasting this time with rebuttals?"

"You jumped ahead in line this morning and demanded attention when the bell had been rung for our announcement, and you were rude. You distracted us and took away from the questions you were asking as if you deserved special attention when you had brought nothing to the table to offer us. You have no respect for rules and boundaries. You need to grow up."

Wolflock gasped, leaning back so far on the cushion that he slipped.

"We are just here to help," Bleen soothed, still smiling with the piercing look that left her eyes cold. "We want you to succeed. You're so clever and you are loved, even if you are obnoxious. You understand that, right?"

Reeling, confused, and feeling like his heart was being crushed, Wolflock could only agree with a nod.

"It is such a relief for you to see sense." Faleen sighed in relief again. "This is the most genuine I have ever seen you and it is such a pleasant change.

"This will ache for a while because you've just had a powerful revelation, but, trust us, it is for the best."

Wolflock nodded numbly again and rose to his feet. "Thank you?"

"Not feeling too raw? These things can leave us with a need to cry and journal some deep reflection."

"I... I think I just need time to process everything."

"That's good. We'll keep an eye out for you. Just don't do any investigating or we'll have to stop you." Bleen tittered.

"Yes. Yes, we will." Faleen's tone had no trace of humour.

Wolflock frowned, laying his hand on the door handle.

"Oh! And one more thing. Please don't discuss your reading with anyone else. Outside influences can taint the results."

He barely glanced back as he left the stuffy room. As the crisp sea air blew around him, Wolflock felt cold. The familiar ship that had been his home felt foreign, like he was seeing a friend after a terrible fight. He didn't think of their warning to not tell anyone about what his reading had entailed, but, at that moment, he didn't care to talk to anyone. Was investigating truly a pipe dream that would be dangerous?

It certainly was dangerous. The person with the knife was an obvious sign of that. But he had done this ever since he could remember. It was his passion. He moved to his room and stood numbly in the middle of it.

He felt so spiritually beaten and bruised that he couldn't muster the anger to combat the pure numbness of his dream being smashed before him. Was music the best path? Had he made this entire journey for naught?

He set the violin on the desk and laid on his bed, staring up at it. When anyone came to the door, he made no answer. He didn't remember sleeping. All he could remember was the feeling that a cherished piece of himself had now been lost.

CHAPTER 3

Serenading the Storm

Wolflock didn't know what time it was. He knew it was dark and that the ship was rolling over the waves more than he'd felt before. He could hear Froderyk being sick in the room across from him. He smelt the thick incense smoke seeping under his door. The memory of the twin's room rippled through his mind and he felt his chest ache. Without thinking, he swung himself out of bed and tore the violin from its smooth wooden case. He found a warm comfort flowing up his arms just from touching it.

Were the twin's predictions true? Was he really

meant to just play music?

The stench of the smoke was suffocating. He couldn't think. Wolflock grasped at the wall as he hauled himself, the violin and bow gripped in his right hand, out into the curtains of rain misting the deck. The crew trotted back and forth across the deck, securing what they could under the huge lantern lights attached to the main masts.

"Take in the halyard, Geagle! And don't let it loose again!" Captain Blutro shouted from the helm. Lightning flashed in front of the ship and Wolflock saw his face in sharpened detail. A few moments later thunder rumbled like a taunting laugh, beckoning them into only Aygir knew what. "Kolor! Get those boxes downstairs or fasten them tight. Smartly now. Tell the others to do the same. We're in for a choppy night."

Wolflock looked at the dining hall door, but he knew someone was bound to be in there and he didn't know what he would say to anyone right now. He slipped around the back of the ship, behind the hall and the helm, looking down at the white crest left in the ship's wake. The grey sea blinked with white light as another flash of lightning pulsed across the sky behind him. Thunder rumbled, low and menacing. The weather was singing to him, and he wanted to pluck a song, but his arm ached in resentment as he tried. He sighed and lowered his arms down, feeling his shoulders and hair soaked by the pitying rain.

"What are yeh doin', lad?" Grogen grabbed his shoulder and turned him about. "Git ta yeh room. Is not safe out 'ere." Wolflock's face must have looked miserable, because Grogen frowned with a deep concern. "Ay, lad. Wha's tha matter?"

Those sympathetic eyes and his emotionally bruised state made Wolflock blurt out, "Have you ever had anyone tell you not to follow your dream? Your calling?"

Grogen smiled sadly and patted his upper arms. "Ah, lad. Now don' you let anyone-"

"Grogen! Are we meant to tie these down or take them downstairs?" Geagle appeared around the corner of the dining hall with two reels of rope on each arm and one loosely around his neck.

"Argh!" the bigger crewman scowled, rushing to yank the reel of rope about Geagle's neck off his body. "Don' be a twit! Never put this 'round yeh neck. You should know better! Tie these boxes tight to the back of the hall."

"They're empty though," Geagle pouted.

"Do yeh wanna take 'em downstairs? No. Didn't

think so. Maybe they'll catch some rainwater."

Wolflock turned back to the water, ignoring the crewmates' argument, and tried to draw up inspiration for a song. If this was meant to be his fate, why resist? Just when he was on the cusp of playing something, Grogen plonked the rope on his shoulder.

"Yeh out of the way back 'ere. Tie yourself off for safety and have a half hour to clear yeh head. Anymore and I'll haul yeh back ta yeh room meself."

"Thank you, Grogen."

The bushy bearded crewmate stopped, his face softening a touch before he turned and made his way back to the crow's nest. Wolflock set to work right away and used one of his newly learned knots around his waist and legs like a climbing harness. At first, he thought to tie himself to the back railing, but if he fell overboard, he didn't fancy hoisting himself back over it.

Geagle had tightly secured the empty crates and barrels at the back of the dining hall. Wolflock could see, in the kitchen light, just through a small window, a decorative rafter that looked very sturdy. He clambered onto the hollow crate under the window, standing wide legged on the edges, and used a tight rolling hitch to keep himself fastened tight, with enough length to just reach the back railing without going over.

The thrill of using his knots practically gave him the energy to play a few short notes. The violin didn't sound tuned anymore. He shook it and water poured out of the swirling holes. He practiced a quick scale and, although the tuning was fine, he felt like it didn't resonate with him. It just sounded... flat. Lifeless.

Anger bubbled up inside him and he angrily plucked the strings. He was being told to lose his calling for investigating, he wouldn't let this stupid pauper's violin try and steal away his music. Wolflock called on his memory for the most furious piece of music he knew, *Presta* by Shoshtakoyevich. After a few bars he growled, scraping the bow so it squealed on the strings. It was too happy. He translated it into a minor key and started again, feeling greater satisfaction from the melancholy insanity that fought against the heavy rain droplets.

He only played for a few minutes when he heard a splash behind the ship. Dolphins! He couldn't make out any pink in the black waters. He played louder, distracted by the potential audience. The ship sliced through a wave as high as the deck and water rushed past his bare feet.

Splash.

It wasn't a dolphin. It was darker.

Splash, splash.

A pod of seals? Wolflock had only read about

them in books. Grey, rotund, agile creatures that looked like dogs that had a desire to be fish. The orange light of the giant lantern shone on the back of the ship, but it wasn't enough to light up the wake while Captain Blutro was using it. Lightning streaked overhead as the wave behind them rose up.

Mermaids!

Wolflock saw them as clear as day in the flash, scattered throughout the wave, their arms pinned tight to their sides and their chubby tails flapping furiously to keep up with the ship. All their giant dark eyes stared unblinking at him. He laughed and whooped, drawing up his bow to give them a good show. *What a sight!*

He sawed his arm back and forth with vigour, finishing *Presta* and going straight into *Sunlight Minuet*. He kept his eyes wide open in the torrential rain as he waited for the next flash of lightning.

The light and the boom of thunder came simultaneously, unveiling his audience from the inky black waters. Again, the flash came and again he played louder and louder. The exhilaration of the ship climbing the waves and soaring down them just made him want to play more. He threw out his memorised material and, in an instant, composed the song of storms and mermaids.

Splash.

A pale shimmer leaped from the wave and fell back into the water.

Flash, Boom!

He saw her. A white mermaid. She streaked through the water faster than the grey ones and reached up to him as she leaped out. She curled her body and flicked her tail playfully, twisting as if she wanted to dance to his music.

So many questions ran through his mind. Why was she white? How did the mermaids hear his music? Could the ship survive the storm? Would Parihaan ever wake up? Who was the person with the knife?

He laughed and played. He held his arms out and cried, "I will always find the answers!"

Flash, Boom!

The mermaids still chased the ship with the albino one at the front. The ship's bow dipped down as it slid down the next wave. It was a huge wave and Wolflock was thankful his rope was fastened tight. Until it slackened.

Flash.

The mermaids were gone except for the albino. Her arm outstretched and her eyes opened wide with fear as if she needed to say something.

Wolflock turned to the kitchen window and saw

someone standing at the window watching him with a hood obscuring their face.

Flash. Boom!

Their gloved hand reached up and slashed his rope with a strange wavy knife as the Silver Ice Hair cut through the wave. The tumultuous water washed over the deck and seized Wolflock around the knees and he collided with the taffrail, tumbling overboard.

His elbow broke the water first, wrenching his shoulder around. His whole body tensed in the freezing darkness, but he had no time to react before a wave tossed him deeper down.

Wolflock choked on the tumbling ice water, the saltwater stinging his eyes. He didn't know which way was up or down. He knew he had to get air. Air. Breathe. Air.

He kicked his legs, grasping the bow and violin as if they would save him. The water buffeted him this way and that, throwing him around like a leaf. It was so cold he didn't realise when he had broken through the surface of the water, coughing and spluttering.

"Help!" he tried to shout, but a wave slapped him back under.

The light of the ship drifted away. They were so much faster than he could swim. He kicked and paddled with the violin until his muscles ached. He was going to drown. If he didn't drown, he was going to freeze. He couldn't. He and Mothy had just found the words.

Appraising Investigator...

He couldn't give up.

As if the sea itself agreed, a wave picked him up and he felt a thick arm wrap around his chest, another gripping his head like a vice. He was held to a body as long as his and whipped through the water, breaking the surface. He coughed again, unable to catch his breath. Were mermaids carnivores? Did they eat humans? Was she going to drown him herself? Was it an act of mercy?

They broke the surface again and he gulped air for a split second before they plunged back under. His hair whooshed over his face with each dive, obscuring his vision. Was she trying to save him?

How would they get onto the ship?

His mind raced, but he was helpless. Her grasp was so powerful that he couldn't move, and she moved so quickly through the water that it was all he could do to breathe when she gave him the chance. He caught the slightest glimpse of the Silver Ice Hair ahead of them and relief spread over his body. She hoisted him up and gripped him tighter, crushing his chest. He coughed and was forced to exhale as she drew up to the back of the ship.

Then she dove into the black water. The lightning flashed and Wolflock could only see emptiness. His lungs burned with the need for air, and the suffocating cold squeezed any strength he had left from his body.

She was going to drown me, he thought as his mind clouded over.

Then she turned and raced in the opposite direction. Her tail beat furiously beyond his naked toes and her powerful body launched them both clear from the height of the wave the ship had just cleared. They plummeted back into the water, falling short of the ship's stern. She crushed his chest again, forcing him to exhale as she dived. This time he was ready. She was trying to launch them onto the back of the ship.

He put up no resistance, but, as she swam up the next huge wave, he kicked with her, hoping it would give them just a bit of a boost.

The wave was higher than the stern of the ship and the mermaid had launched them at just the right angle. Wolflock saw the light of the ship through his hair and the water as they hurtled towards the deck, but the ship moved forward over the next wave.

They hit one of the fastened crates, and everything went dark.

CHAPTER 4

Wolflock's Wet White Knight

Wolflock couldn't feel anything. It was if a blanket of burning butterflies were shrouding him. He could hear the slosh of water right by his ear. He heard dull footsteps trampling along the deck. He couldn't open his eyes. Did he have eyes anymore? Was he a spectre cursed to forever haunt the ship after his watery demise?

He felt a firm pressure around his chest. Was he

drowning again?

He heard the slosh of water and felt someone with a broad webbed glove hold his head up.

"Wolflock!" someone shouted. He couldn't tell who.

I'm right here. Why are you yelling?

"Wolflock?" another person called.

"This isn't funny, Mr Felen," Captain Blutro shouted. He was right in front of him.

I'm here, Captain. Why do you sound so displeased? Did you find the beetroot dye for Aujin?

"Lockie! Lockie! Where are you?"

Hearing Mothy's voice crack brought on a surge of energy from Wolflock. He used all his willpower to crack open his eyes and speak as loud as he could.

"M-Mothy," he whispered.

The footsteps passed him.

"Mothy!" he groaned a little louder. The person holding him tried to lift him and purred a bubbling sound in his ear.

"Lockie!"

He saw the blonde hair and crystal green eyes peek into the crate. He smiled. He was safe. Mothy would take care of him. Wolflock couldn't keep his eyes open, but he could hear everything in strange waves. As if the conductor of all noises was telling the orchestra to raise and lower the volume every few seconds.

"Please help me," Mothy groaned, heaving Wolflock's waterlogged body from the deep crate. The leathery hands gave him a shove and the person in the crate crawled out with a wet slap on the deck before they wrapped their arms around his chest again. "I've found him! Captain! I've found him!"

"Quickly! To the kitchen. He's as blue as glaciers."

"Smartly now, Mothy, me lad."

"She won't let him go." Mothy pulled under Wolflock's arms. The air was blistering against his wet clothes. "Please help us move him, Miss. Please!"

With the same bubbling purr, the woman holding him around the chest let him go. Her feet must have been exceptionally large because every limping step she took sounded like a slap on the deck. The bustling around him was frantic, but Wolflock felt fine. So sleepy. Mothy untied the rope still around his waist and thighs, stripped off his wet clothes under the Captain's orders and Grogen wrapped him in a towel by the kitchen fire, cradling him like a child. The woman kept her cool arms wrapped around his exposed leg. It was the first time he realised how horrible her stench was. Like someone had woven a warm, wet blanket out of fish guts.

"It's all well. We've found him. Go about your normal day," Goden told someone by the door.

"Is he in good health? Can we see him?" Tanni, the widowed mother, asked from the entrance.

"Please, I may be able to assist," Nü pleaded.

"No, no. He's fine. We know how to treat chilled bones on the ship. Go back to your business. No need for a spectacle."

"Where is he?"

"Is there really a mermaid?"

"We must see him!" Bleen and Faleen demanded.

Wolflock heard a scuffle and lifted his weighted eyelids enough to see the warm glow of the kitchen fire. His bleary vision caught the frame of a ghostly figure at his leg. Two bright pink eyes blinked up at him.

"You..." he wheezed, his face creaking into a half smile.

"Lockie!" Mothy gasped and hugged his friend, squashing him more into Grogen's chest. The huge crewmate was sniffling. "What happened? Why were you in the box? What were you thinking?"

He felt Mothy shake his arm through the blanket, but all he could do was move his eyes to look up at his faithful friend and try to convey that he couldn't make another utterance.

"We knew it!" Bleen cried triumphantly.

"He needs rest! Yeh can't barge in here-"

"We told him if he continued his path of prying into sleuthing work that he would put himself in grave danger," Faleen snorted.

"You tried to make up your mind and the universe gave you a resounding sign to help you," Bleen stroked his wet hair. "We knew you would resist but I'm so pleased that the energies putting you in your correct place have left you undamaged. I knew they would."

"We knew they would."

"He knows his right path is that of music. Look. I even found the violin and bow just next to the box he was cocooned up in. Now you can emerge like a beautiful butterfly."

Wolflock scrunched his face in distaste. He didn't want her to touch him.

"Is tha' what yeh told him that left him so miserable on the deck last night!" Grogen roared. "You told 'im not ta follow 'is dreams, did yeh!? He couldn' 'ave been more morose if someone had died! You pair 'ave a lot ta answer for!"

The mermaid made a hissing and spitting noise, like she was trying to bring up phlegm. It made such a sharp, high noise that Bleen flinched away.

"It's a wild mermaid, Ms Quaretz. Please leave now. You may relay any fortunes to Mr Felen after he has recovered and is willing." Captain Blutro's stern voice left no room for argument.

"Yes, Captain. Perhaps playing him some music would assist his recovery."

Wolflock didn't know if they spoke again or left immediately, but he was glad for the silence. All that could be heard was the crackle of the fireplace and the occasional sniff from Grogen as he held the freezing boy to his chest. Time crept by like a sea snail and Wolflock felt himself begin to shiver, waking him out of sleep. Mothy pressed a warm ginger tea into his hands and Grogen insisted that he eat some of Goden's best pastries with the sweetest filling.

"C-c-cardamon," Wolflock insisted through chattering teeth. He needed something to break up the sweet flavour. The mermaid made a high-pitched yawning sound, smacking her lipless mouth. "And f-f-f-fish for h-her?"

Mothy laughed and presented her with one of the fish from the window by kneeling down on one knee as if he were presenting the King with a sacred sword.

She made three high squeaks and rested her long-fingered hand on the fish, raising it up pinched between two short black webbed claws. She opened her sharp toothed mouth wide and swallowed it whole. As she ate, Wolflock took a moment to observe her. Her blubbery body and thick arms jiggled with every movement she made, and she preferred to lay prostrated on her stomach, hands tucked under her chest. Her pink eyes boggled out of her face, possibly allowing for more telescopic vision, and the shape of her face was drawn forward like a seal. Her flat nose sported nostrils that flared open with each breath. Her ears were tiny and sat higher on her skull than a human's. The little ears poked out of her braided white hair. Amongst the braids were shining black shells that seemed to resemble eyes. Her ears moved back and forth depending on the direction she wanted to listen and appeared to be able to move independently. If all of this hadn't astounded Wolflock enough, her alabaster skin with mottled grey and yellow flecks made her look celestial.

"Your new girlfriend is pretty," Mothy snickered, rubbing Wolflock's black hair with a kitchen towel.

"I-I'm ch-ch-choosing t-to ignore that-t-t," he shivered. "Sh-she s-s-aved my l-life."

"She's a rare one. I've never seen a pale mermaid," whispered Grogen. "I can' tell if yeh cursed or blessed, Wolflock."

"I'd say both," Mothy and Wolflock said at the same time.

The three of them chuckled and the mermaid looked around for more fish. Eventually Wolflock's shivering subsided, and he felt exhausted, but warm. The entrance to the dining hall opened and Captain Blutro strode in with Slavidus.

"Ah! Excellent. Thank goodness you're well again. How on Pelaia did you end up in that crate with a mermaid, Mr Felen?" Captain Blutro chortled and knelt next to Mothy.

"Mermaid?" Slavidus stopped and stayed well back behind the kitchen bench between the dining hall and cooking area. "Why hasn't she been put back? Quickly now!"

"She has been rather attached to our Wolflock here, it appears," Captain Blutro said.

"Yes, but-"

"You're welcome to try and move her."

"Don' do it now. Her pods prob'ly long gone."

"That's not the issue right now. Mr Felen, did you honestly go out on the deck last night without securing yourself?"

"No sir. I tied myself to that rafter through the window. I... I think someone must not have realised what it was for and untied it."

"Hmm...Or you need more practice on your knots." The captain said as if he wasn't convinced, although Wolflock couldn't tell about what. "When you're well I will insist that you retake your lessons. No knot tied by my crew should be escapable unless intended to be so."

Something about his tone emphasised the point to Wolflock, but he still didn't understand what he meant.

"That's all well and good, but what are we doing about her?" Slavidus insisted.

"I-I w-want to make sure she well fed a-and I'm sure we can s-s-send her on her way."

Wolflock's words made the older men look uncomfortable. Finally, the captain spoke up.

"It has been too long, Wolflock. Her pod hasn't been following us and is likely to be miles away now. If we release her in the middle of the sea without the protection of her pod, she will be attacked by sharks or orcas."

"Is it because she's d-d-different?"

"Precisely. Her abnormality makes her special, but also vulnerable."

"Can we a-attract her pod to us? Or f-find it for her?"

"Her family's likely heading to Creast for the Pisces moon. Tha people hold a big celebration and tha bay gets filled with mermaids and fish. Tha's over a week away though."

"Perhaps we can keep her on as a special guest until then?" Mothy shrugged and fed her an olive by throwing it in the air. She caught it with a powerful thud of her jaws.

"No! No. Definitely not. Captain you're not seriously thinking about this?"

Captain Blutro stroked his short beard in thought, then raised an eyebrow at Slavidus's consternation. "Speak frankly, what would be your objection?"

"You know having sea creatures out of land is bad luck. What if she calls for her pod, and they think she's been captured and sinks the ship? What if she eats one of the men? They're meant to be in the water, and it makes me awfully uncomfortable to have her on board. It's as simple as that."

Wolflock heard an odd inflection in his voice, and he saw Slavidus fold his hand under his shirt as if he were hiding something. Captain Blutro had seen it too.

"Let's go have a chat. Mr Felen has been through enough. I leave him in your charge Grogen."

Mothy cleared his throat loudly.

"And in your charge too, Mothy."

The two leaders of the ship departed, and the dining hall fell silent. Mothy placed Wolflock's wet clothes on the oven to dry. Grogen insisted on him drinking three large cups of ginger tea over the hour, before Mothy passed the dry, crispy warm clothes back for Wolflock to dress.

"Why doesn't Slavidus like mermaids?" he blurted out. He felt a sting of indignation that Slavidus was abjectly rude to the creature that had saved his life.

"Not a clue. Weird ta be honest. Not a crew member on board would think poorly of a mermaid. 'Spose he just got shocked seeing one up close. Not many get that privilege. I don't think he's been particular fond of 'em ever, though. After seein' how she ate that fish, I can sorta understand."

"Perhaps. Regardless, we have to help her get back to her pod or convince Slavidus to let her stay on til Creast. Would it be possible to inform all of the crew mates on crow's nest duty to keep a keen watch out and bring it immediately to my attention?"

Grogen sighed with relief. "It's good ta see yeh well so fast. Yes, I can tell 'em all ta keep an eye out. Yeh 'ave to promise me though, don' be doin' anythin' strenuous, aye? No big mischief today, aye?"

Wolflock smiled darkly. "I think my body would protest as much as you, Grogen. No, no. One bout of hypothermia is enough. I will rest. Perhaps I'll just spend the day reading as I recover. How tight of a schedule are we on to reach our next destination?"

"Irid is on the North West shore and is 'bout two to three days off. Why?"

"I was hoping we'd have more time. No matter. Judging by the Captain's confusion at Slavidus' superstitious objections to our mermaid friend's presence on the ship, I'm suspecting that he will give us until Irid to find her family." Wolflock paced back and forth in front of the fire, pinching his chin with the blanket still cuddled around his torso. "This means that if we rely solely on the chance that the watch will spy our quarry, we are unlikely to succeed."

"Beggin' yeh pardon, Wolflock, but our crow's nest watch has keen eyes as yeh asked for."

"I understand that Grogen, but I am coming to find I prefer to reduce the risk of a gamble. It may very well be that the crew spot her pod and we can reunite them with little effort. Given the hypothesised time restraints, I'd prefer to put in a little extra effort to accomplish the task."

"Come sickness or threats of death, nothing stops

you, does it, Lockie?" Mothy chuckled.

Wolflock smirked back at him before continuing. "Grogen, would you know if the ship has details on the mermaid migration path and the ship's plotted voyage?"

"Tha's a question for the Cap'in. He's got all the books, maps, notes, and what nots yeh'd be after. It's nothin' I've paid much mind to."

"Well, best we speak to him." Wolflock charged to the door, hearing the mermaid following him. He stopped and turned, not hearing Mothy follow too.

"Are you not coming?"

Mothy shuffled his feet and avoided Wolflock's gaze, "I... umm... I was going to get my... reading..."

"What? Oh. Why?"

"I just thought it would still be fun, ya know? Maybe... I dunno. Anyway, you go on and see the Captain. I'll meet you there soon."

Wolflock felt himself spark with irritation, but he couldn't articulate why. He pressed his lips together in a flat line and opened the door to the blistering wind outside. "Yes. Well. I'll see you."

The fresh air cooled the strange heat that had arisen in him as he made his way down into the passenger cabins. The mermaid wiggled backwards down the stairs, never leaving his side for a moment. She sniffed eagerly at everything and ran her webbed hands over all the grey wood. If she could pick up anything, she put it in her mouth to chew on. She did this with a coiled rope, a barrel lid, the stair railing, and a decorative plaque that had fallen from the wall in the storm.

"Are you hungry? What can and can't you eat? Let me get my shoes and we'll do a bit of research on just that."

He ducked into his room, pulled on dry socks, shoes and his jacket, pocketed his journal, and guided the mermaid to the Captain's quarters. He moved to knock on the door, but, as he could hear voices, he decided to let them finish. The mermaid blinked up at him with her giant pink eyes and purred, tugging firmly at the hem of his jacket with her sharp fingers. Wolflock smiled and squatted down so she could get a better look.

"You don't really wear clothes, do you? Is it your blubber that keeps you warm in this freezing weather? Southern mermaids are all drawn as being slender and a bit more fish like. You're a bit more like a seal. We only see tiny little seals in the rivers in Grothener." Her skin looked like it was lifting on her shoulder. He reached out to make sure it wasn't an unattended injury and found dense coarse fur that was so compact it looked like skin. "Incredible. No wonder the cold doesn't bother you.

What a fascinating creature."

"Blrr beh cruh creh," she gurgled back at him.

Wolflock blinked. "You can speak? Or make articulated noises I should say."

Entranced, Wolflock didn't notice the door open behind him.

"Mr Felen?" Captain Blutro asked as Slavidus stormed past, leaping aside to keep as much distance as possible between him and the mermaid. "I was just about to find you."

"To tell me you've decided that I have until Irid to find the mermaid's pod?" Wolflock dusted his sleeves.

Captain Blutro's face grew exasperated. "How-"

"Slavidus didn't walk out happily, so she's not being put back in the water immediately. He also didn't look too frightened, which would have suggested that she was permitted to stay on until Creast and bring this superstitious prediction to a terrible fruition in his mind. He looked annoyed and dodged away from her as one does when you have to tolerate something for just a bit longer. I have done the same thing with my sister when she is being particularly petulant."

"Interesting deductions, I have said two evenings. Then, regardless of the circumstances, we will place her back in the wild."

"What if we can find her pod sooner by changing our course?"

The captain exhaled and waved them both into his room. "Open the door to the balcony lad. She smells awful."

"I think I must be getting used to the smell."

"I don't want her making my good sheets and antique journals smell like rotten fish and seaweed. Now, I know you must be hatching some plan to assist her. I can understand your desire. She saved your life." The captain sat at his desk as the mermaid made her way to the balcony and stared out at the wake of the ship. "We have lost a few hours stopping the ship to search for you this morning. I would have been a week late if it meant saving your life, although it would have cost me my ship and crew. But we are in a pickle."

Wolflock took a seat across from him on the plush blue and grey chair.

"We have medicines onboard that are urgent for an outbreak of pneumonia at Irid. The doctors sent word to the Krieger Zwerg post office for us. We're the fastest vessel that can travel this late in the season. We can't afford to delay. Your life is saved, but we can only offer your friend passage to the shore. She'll be able to find her way quickly to Creast for the Pisces Moon festival."

The tone of his voice didn't sound convincing to Wolflock. "Unless?"

The Captain's dark eyes flicked towards him. "I don't want to put terrible thoughts into your head. Mermaids are very smart. They're resourceful, they can use tools and, from the little we know of them, they can navigate. You never see a lone mermaid, though. Well..."

"The suspense does not endear me to your plan so far, Captain."

"Sometimes wild orcas will eat mermaids, especially if they've mistaken them for a seal or a walrus."

"What's an orca?"

"A huge black and white whale that is dolphin shaped without the nose. They're incredibly clever and we've never had a record of them eating a human. In fact, we have records of them helping humans hunt in the harder months. There are records of them being at some kind of war with mermaids, though."

"What records are you referring to?"

"I'm glad you asked. All the books in this bookcase," he gestured to his left to the shelves filled with various textbooks, "are instructional. They are filled with all things every ship's crew needs to know. All the parts of a ship, the currents in the waters we travel, food preparation, rationing, navigating, games and history.

There are also a few mythology texts and general flora and fauna books that may keep you entertained. If you can find a place that corresponds with our navigation and the mermaids' migration, we will drop her off there and let her follow her own path. Give me an hour to prepare the books you should need, and you can begin your investigation with your friends."

The word 'investigation' rang like a clear bell through Wolflock's mind, and he bit his lip thinking of what the twins had said.

"If I may, Captain. Please don't tell anyone I'm investigating anything. Or, perhaps, don't think of it as an investigation at all?"

Captain Blutro peered at him with narrowed eyes. "Hmm... As you wish, Mr Felen. Would you prefer the term research? Or mermaid-minding?"

"Research is acceptable."

Wolflock looked over at the mermaid, happily flipping her tail back and forth as she gazed out over the railing, her squishy chin resting on her hands. "Two nights, you say? Starting tonight?"

"That is the agreement."

He nodded, still looking at the mermaid in the afternoon sun. "Lucky I'm a quick study then."

CHAPTER 5
Researching the Myth

Wolflock had to give the captain time to secure any sensitive documents and organise his office. To pass the time, he took the mermaid back onto the top deck to try and find her some food. As he collected samples from the kitchen, he found she would nibble on anything, but would spit out spiced foods, and ate meat pieces whole. He was only disturbed when Yifi came inside to ask Matroos for a cup of tea as he prepared dinner.

"Lavender, if it isn't too much trouble, Matroos," she said politely, glancing at the mermaid who watched her unblinkingly.

"One pot of lavender tea, coming up," he hummed in response.

Yifi stared back at Himi. "Is she safe?"

"She hasn't displayed any signs of discomfort or sickness from being out of the water, so I assume she's fine."

"No, no. I meant, does she bite?"

Wolflock stared. Perhaps it was her lack of expression, but he could see that Yifi spoke about her as if she were an unknown dog or horse. He knew she was a 'creature', but he didn't think she was unintelligent.

"She hasn't harmed me or anyone who has gotten too close," he sniffed, ignoring how she'd growled at Bleen.

"She's so... extraordinary. And flexible!" Yifi smiled, kneeling down, and holding out her hand. "The mermaids near Corl are stiff and streamlined. Like marlin. Does she have a name?"

Wolflock frowned. "Do you have a name?"

The mermaid looked up at him as he spoke, then back at Yifi.

"Wolflock," he pressed his hand to his chest, then gestured to her. "Wolflock."

Yifi blinked up at him, "Does she speak?"

"In a way. Wolflock, and you?"

The aroma of boiling lavender slinked around them as they continued to prompt her to speak. Finally, she put her hand to her own chest and made a drawn-out humming gurgle.

"Hrrmmgleh An."

Yifi jumped back and Wolflock laughed.

"Huurummgeh."

"Ah. The dialect is peculiar. Unfortunately, I remained unskilled in such throaty languages. We might have to go with a nickname."

"Hrrmi," she touched her chest and reached out to Wolflock. "Uurf gluk."

"Himi? Himi. Wolflock. Himi. Wolflock," he repeated back and forth a few times, making her purr in short bursts that sounded like giggles.

"This is incredible. I never..." Yifi breathed, "How did you know she could speak?"

"She did earlier. Her hair is braided with shells woven into it. If my sister has taught me anything, it's that women who do their hair with such intricacy enjoy a good chat with the hair stylist."

Yifi laughed. "This is true. Do you think she'll let me touch her?"

Before Wolflock could respond to her question,

the door to the dining hall opened. Veluse the artist slumped into the room, dragging his feet. His normally buoyant, auburn hair drooped flat on his scalp and his downcast eyes seemed to have lost their sparkle. Tanni followed soon after, wearing her beaded mourning veil, which he hadn't seen in some time, with a similarly dejected slump.

"Who is the lavender tea for?" Wolflock watched as all the crew and company that came through the door to afternoon tea looked exhausted, melancholy, or deep in thought.

"Dlumi and Nü." Yifi said as she reached out to touch Himi's tail. Just before she stroked it, Himi flopped it away.

"What are they upset about?"

"Huh? How did you know they were upset?"

"Lavender tea is for soothing nerves, calming nightmares, and relieving anxiety. It's one that everyone in the central regions of Puinteyle would know. Why do they need the tea?"

Yifi blushed. "They... they didn't ask for it. I just wanted to help. I heard them both crying in their rooms. Well. Dlumi was in her room. Nü was in Parihaan's room."

"And you don't need it as well? I take it they had...

profound fortunes read? You've also had yours done today too?" Wolflock frowned.

"How did you know?"

"You have the lingering smell of the same incense smoke in your hair, and I could see the stain of the cliffberry tea on your teeth. Why are you unperturbed?"

"I never put much stock in fortunes. My mother was an actual witch, and we've fought with many charlatans over the years. Especially when they took our regular clients."

"That's all, is it?" He raised an eyebrow, noting her rolling a plain pewter ring on her middle left finger.

"A lady must have her secrets against any negative powers and unseen forces," she winked.

"You don't think the twins are able to make true predictions, do you?"

Yifi gasped as Himi flopped her tail onto her hand to get attention.

"She's so soft! Hello there, Himi." Yifi stroked her tail gingerly. "Aren't you amazing?"

Before he could ask her to elaborate, Mothy came into the hall with the same downcast look. Wolflock couldn't stand for that. He took determined steps up to his slumping friend and grasped his shoulders.

"I'm so glad you're here." He cupped Mothy's face

and turned his eyes up. "We have much to discuss."

"You're clear." Mothy frowned as if he were in a daze.

"What?"

"Uh. Sorry. You're here. The incense in the room makes your head foggy, doesn't it?"

"It does, indeed. How did you go? Would you like some tea?"

Mothy's helpless face made Wolflock outraged. It was one thing for the twins to tell him he couldn't follow his path and pursue his goals, but to have upset his dear friend in this manner was unforgivable.

"Wolflock," he swallowed and pulled at his sleeve. "We... We can't... I mean..."

Wolflock eyes steeled, and he steered Mothy to the kitchen bench, pressing one of Yifi's lavender teas into his hands.

"What did they tell you?" he whispered, looking into his friend's tragic blue eyes.

Mothy rolled the cup in his hands. "I'm not meant to say. I don't think anyone is."

"They told me not to say either, but I'll fight the gods if they get in my way so allow me to be the exception you need."

Mothy laughed through his nose and held the cup

to his chest.

"I have spent more energy making myself an agreeable acquaintance to all on board, I'm not about to let a bit of hocus pocus spoil all my hard work. And believe me, it was awfully hard work."

Mothy finally let out a small chuckle and took a sip. It was as if the more contact was made between the two of them, the more the fogginess around him lifted.

"Besides, you are the only human friend I've genuinely had. If I lost you, I don't know what I would do."

Mothy's face brightened, and his usual smile returned. "Being tumbled through the sea and coming close to death has made you either wise or kind."

"As if I wasn't both already," he scoffed.

"Umm... Wolflock?" Yifi choked from the floor. "Help."

The boys looked down at Himi laying across Yifi, braiding her chestnut hair.

After causing a stir removing the mermaid from the maiden, Wolflock ordered more lavender tea. He glared around the room at the depressed company and slammed a mug of tea down in front of each person while Yifi introduced Himi to Mothy formally.

"Drink," he growled to anyone who looked

questioningly at him. Once he felt he had done justice to correct the energy of the room, he stalked back to Mothy. "Now. Let's hear what they told you so I can rectify it."

The room went from quiet to silent and Wolflock felt everyone watching them.

Mothy sipped the rest of his tea and set the cup down. "I need to think things over first. I don't even want to write down what they told me in case it comes true." He paused for a moment and frowned around the room. After a deep breath, he sat up straight and braced his shoulders. "I will tell you. Just not yet. Soon, though."

The company seemed to hold their breath. Himi made a low growl and whine, sensing the tension.

"Very well. Our next point of business, though. How are we going to keep a fully grown mermaid fed and happy for two nights, Mothy?"

"That is not full grown," Matroos's deep bass voice commented as he laid out a tray of delicately decorated fish rolls with dill and yoghurt sauce. "She's a baby."

"Baby? She's bigger than me, though!" Wolflock said.

"Shiriling mermaids get bigger the further North you go. Some of them get as wide as a tonne-barrel. She's maybe... six or eight summers old."

"That's so fascinating." said Mothy.

"And, like any child, you entertain them with music, games and food." Matroos plonked a bowl of disgusting fish scraps in front of them. "You're going to have an educational few days, boys." he grinned.

Himi reached up and pulled the bowl down, crashing it to the ground and scoffing the fish scraps. Wolflock leaped away, disgusted by the fresh pungent smell.

"Music sounds much better. Mothy! Get your drum. I need some fresh air."

After arguing with Mothy to leave the rest of the fish guts for Matroos to clean up, the three of them made their way onto the deck under the grey sky. Wolflock sat on the ground looking between the railing, feeling safer not being above it, and watching the water for any movement while Mothy made up silly songs for Himi. He hoped that while they waited for word from the Captain about their research resources, that they could summon the dolphins again and possibly the mermaids. The fresh sea air washed away all but the present anxieties of getting Himi home.

Wolflock closed his tired eyes and took a deep breath, falling into a light sleep. As the sun sat on the horizon, masked by the thick clouds, Wolflock woke just enough to become aware of the movements on the ship.

Nan Ji was in a deep discussion with his tearful daughter while Tinni and the boys played mah-jong beside them. The crew were moving some of the container's downstairs, emptying the rainwater into the drinking water barrels. The people milling around the deck seemed to be in a far better mood than the people who had retreated into the dining hall. He opened his eyes when Mothy stopped drumming and Himi laid her tail across Wolflock's lap, her head on his feet.

"What?" Wolflock looked up at his friend.

"You look so peaceful there. I'm going to get you a blanket."

"I'm fine."

"No, no. I'm going to do it. Wait here. I might even get Veluse to paint you. It's the most serene I ever see you and I want to capture it."

If Himi hadn't been laying on him, Wolflock thought he would have given Mothy a shove for that comment. He patted her smelly tail and smiled. He would find a way to get her home. There had to be clues others before him hadn't put together. He would investigate everything.

Appraising Investigator.

The words still resounded in his chest like a deep drumbeat. He felt the path before him becoming clear, exciting, and rich with adventure. There were no constraints from the rigid societies of Plugh. No monotony. He could see himself travelling, learning, and making choices for himself. He wouldn't be beholden to his father. To an agent. To an employer. He'd be free. He could conduct experiments that might further the discovery skills of the Guard, the keepers of law and order in Puinteyle. He could find missing items and solve the puzzles no one else could solve. He had been called to follow this path ever since he was a child. How could he ever turn his back on it?

The ear-piercing shriek of someone playing the violin atrociously wrenched him from his thoughts. As he sat up, he caught a whiff of overbearing incense as Bleen, and her dark purple shroud of hair, bounced into view. She was pretending to play his violin in a mocking fashion.

Faleen stood stiff and tall behind her, looking down her nose as always.

"Ah. I wish I could make it sing like you do. How are you feeling, Wolflock?" Bleen simpered, kneeling next to him, but keeping her distance from the lightly snoring Himi.

"I'm fine."

"Oh, that is so good to hear. We were so worried

about you. What has the Captain said about your new pet?" She smiled down at Himi, but it didn't reach her eyes. Faleen stood back, arms crossed, pretending not to listen.

Wolflock didn't speak for a moment. He felt hazy. His mind clouded and he didn't know whether to tell the truth or not.

"The Captain asked Mothy and I to help look after her until he makes a decision." Not the whole truth, but not an outright lie.

"Ah. We could tell poor Slavidus is so hurt by this creature being allowed on board. We do hope he gets his resolution quickly. It's a shame the captain has put you in this situation again. I hope it's just to keep a watchful eye and not to think too hard on anything. We know it's hard for you to break out of your patterns, but it is going to be much better for you in the long run."

Bleen touched his shoulder delicately and Himi's eyes snapped open. Her mouth opened just enough to bare two rows of razor-sharp round teeth. Wolflock was relieved for the disruption.

"Ahem. Anyway. We found this in the kitchen. It told me it missed you greatly. Your new pet might even benefit from a song or two. I know the ship would." Bleen giggled as she passed the violin to him, pressing it into his hands.

Is she saying that because the ship's mood lifts when I play or because it will show everyone that they should follow your rules?

"Thank you," was all he uttered, taking the violin and bow from her.

"You play beautifully. The power of our readings have left several people revaluating their lives thoroughly. It is excellent to see their transformations into what they ought to be. They would benefit from your playing. Bleen will organise a concert for you." Faleen still averted her eyes as if anything else on the ship was more interesting than talking to Wolflock.

"Oh yes! I have organised many a concert for the noble houses across the continent. It would be my-"

"Himi, off please." Wolflock rose, feeling suffocated by the smoky smell emanating from the twins. "That won't be necessary, Bleen. I'm quite tired and have no mood to play for everyone. If you'll excuse me."

Bleen stammered as he walked away, Himi, growling, in tow. He made a point of making fierce eye contact with Faleen to show her that she hadn't broken his spirit. Her violet eyes were wide with something akin to shock and rage. It brought him the utmost satisfaction that she blinked first as he walked on by. It was small, but it felt like a triumph.

As he made his way down into the cabins, he bumped into Mothy and Captain Blutro talking. The Captain waved them into his study, where piles of books were laid out by category.

"I never thought we'd have anyone interested in these books. Most of the crew learn on the job and I only used books like these in my early training. It's good to see them finally opened," the captain commented as Wolflock dived between the piles, searching for the ones with the most up to date maps.

There were twelve textbooks and five sets of differently coloured journals. Five brown, seventeen green, twenty-eight faded blue, sixteen red, and sixteen black.

"I'm on evening duty, so come and speak with me at the helm if you need to. Oh, and please keep the windows open tonight. I'd rather not sleep amongst the smell of mermaid in the morning."

Mothy chuckled, but Wolflock barely acknowledged the Captain after burying his face in one of the larger books.

The hours passed slowly by the fairy dust lantern light. Every time it dimmed, Mothy would show Himi how to shake it up and set it down gently on top of

Wolflock's largest stack of read books. This proved disastrous at one point as Wolflock yanked a previous book out to cross reference a point on sea currents, and the lanterns toppled down. Himi caught it on her tail and flicked Wolflock with her webbed fingers in a chastising fashion.

Mothy was her favourite form of entertainment as he chose to read the biological books on mermaids and local fauna out loud to her. She made different noises, pointing at each picture, and slapping her hands on the ground when she got excited.

Wolflock was undistracted. His long nose remained buried in the books mapping the sea. Weather patterns, historical trades, battles, scientific advancement. Wolflock's piercing blue eyes raced across the lines on the old pages and he paid no courtesy to how roughly he turned them.

"This is ridiculous," he snapped after several hours of scrutinising the books. He slammed shut *Tartanus Fiergo's 'The Silver Lake: Making the Mutable Immutable'*. "Half of these people have never even been on the water! This pretentious fool thinks that, by getting drunk with the bureaucrats of the local areas, he could put together this drivel. And this one just liked how pretty the water was, but couldn't swim, was terrified of sailing and hated fish! It's all well and good to say they believe there are volcanic openings under the water and that's why the river system is so rich. But where is the description of the currents weaving like seaweed being blown back and forth by the breath of the ocean? Where is the practicality?"

Mothy and Himi eyed each other nervously at his outburst. "Uh... well, this one has an idea that mermaids follow the same migration patterns as dolphins around this time of the year?" he offered with a shrug.

"Hrm meh jehm," Himi barked, sliding over to Wolflock to watch him read.

"I feel like it would be more effective to just ask the crew what stories they'd learned in their travels. There are a lot of pieces of artwork onboard depicting mermaids. I haven't seen any like Himi though. They all seem to be Southern mermaids."

"I heard earlier that every night until we hit the ice will be rough, so we can't go and ask them now. Maybe some of the journals will help us?" Mothy shrugged and pulled a leather-bound set of green journals to his side, flicking through them.

Wolflock sighed and did the same with a grey set that was still tinged with the hint of blue it used to be.

It didn't take long before Mothy started fading. He

stretched, cat-like, and stood up, pacing with the book in hand before tilting his head to the ceiling.

"Go and get food." Wolflock huffed. "You're no use to me tired, and your inability to keep focused is starting to distract me."

Mothy bit his lip and glanced between Wolflock and the door.

"Are you sure-"

"You may also want to tell Nü, Haatji and Geagle what is going on as well. We'll need extra time to take our shifts watching Parihaan so we can move our research materials into the room."

"Thank the sea! I'll be back with food." Mothy sighed in relief, dashing from the room.

Wolflock shook his head and stared after his friend with a cold look. Mothy hadn't found anything of use and Wolflock was tempted to go over his work to make sure he hadn't missed anything important. With a sigh he thought to himself that he'd go through Mothy's books last.

The thought that Mothy may be going back to speak with Faleen and Bleen burned through his mind, only soothed when Himi rested her head on his shin.

"You're right. This is about getting you home. Not Mothy wanting a stupid psychic reading."

Any book he finished, he passed to Himi to palm through. It was nice to have company while he studied. Better than his little sister Myna constantly reading over his shoulder saying, "Finished. Turn the page. Why are you so slow? This book is boring. Have you figured it out yet? I have."

Captain Blutro's great, great grandfather's journals were so dull. Regular logs, only names and cargo. Nothing interesting at all. He didn't bother finishing it and tossed it to Himi.

"Hrm meh jehm!"

He looked up. She had opened the book at the back and pointed to an intricate drawing of a Shiriling mermaid.

"What?" Wolflock snatched the book back. Old Captain Lothran Silk had flipped his book around and written about mermaids.

... their shimmering hair, long and flowing, only marks their confidence as apex creatures of the sea, as, like with land humans, they can afford to be ostentatious at the risk of safety...

...Do not feed them cliff berries. Not because they make them sick, but because they are addictive and

aggravating to them...

...I believe I am learning their language. It very closely resembles the ancient Shirth tongue, but, due to the broad shape of their mouths and indiscernible lips, they pronounce things in their throats....

...I saw the giant octopus again. I await the next sighting of mermaids shortly, or, as I believe they call themselves, 'hafmeyjam'...

... I followed the exact same route, yet no view of them this journey...

... I've noted sharks and dolphins, but no octopus, yet the stars say we are in the correct location. The crew wish for me to weigh anchor, but I want to wait just a few more hours...

... We located a warm patch of water when Billjork fell into the water and didn't freeze instantly. A day later we hit the current we expected and sped to Irid faster than ever before. The crew said they thought they saw whale footprints, but it was some kind of heat source...

...That's it. The heat and cold make the currents weave, cross and swirl. It's like ribbons. The sea is too big to map, but we know the signs... The Silver Ice Hair can follow them. When they freeze, the currents leave great tracks of smooth ice for us to sail on for miles at top speed....

... Had to leave Mrogen on land at Creast. He was fishing and snagged a mermaid. I hope he got away and his pod cut him free. He was out of sight before we lowered the lifeboat to help. I told Mrogen no fishing after we've seen dolphins. I won't have them hurt the mermaids again. It's a bad omen...

...I glimpsed it today. I'm sure of it! Sinalta stood on the horizon like a blue topaz. We saw mermaids again, if only briefly. I feel an ache in my heart that this may be the last time...

His journal was dated, and the location marked for each entry. It appeared that every nine years he would see the mermaids themselves, but, in the other years, he would still see some kind of sign. Whether that was coincidence or not was still undetermined.

Wolflock felt as if he had the threads of his mental

web laid out before him. He took a piece of large paper from the Captain's desk and drew the map of the Hatfjorn Sea, plotting the path the Silver Ice Hair was set to take to Irid, then to Creast. He marked the spot where they had seen dolphins, where he supposed they had seen mermaids, and then, with a pencil, began speculating where Old Captain Lothran had found the heated vents. He corresponded his map with the static map from Tartanus and several of the old stories.

He hated having to guess, but, with each one, he had only a general radius of where the currents flowed, where mermaids had been sighted, where other animals had been sighted, and the suspected locations of Sinalta.

The more he read through the journals, the more Sinalta was mentioned. Biologists suspected that it wasn't a place of myth, but rather the secret child rearing grounds of the Shiriling mermaids. He ran his hands through his hair, gripping it to collect his thoughts. There were no mermaid migration paths that lined up with the rest of their journey because the currents had changed. But he didn't feel hopeless. Not by any stretch. In fact, Wolflock's heart beat hard in his chest with excitement. The more of the journals he read, the more things came together.

"There are signs," he muttered to himself, adding

another current to his map. "They're everywhere, Himi. Animals, currents, seasons. It's all here. Old man Lothran may have given up, but I won't!"

Mothy opened the door to the Captain's study with a tray of seed bread, clam chowder and six full fish for Himi. Wolflock saw him pause and look at the ink stained, dishevelled sleuth with concern.

"Mothy!" He breathed with a crazed smile. "Mothy I've solved it! We're not going to find her pod."

Mothy set the dinner tray down on the ornate desk and looked at the scribbled map. "That doesn't sound like solving it."

"No, you don't understand! We're not going to find her pod because what we're doing is taking her directly home. We're going to find Sinalta!"

CHAPTER 6
A Franz Gudderwiest Original

Mothy raised a sceptical eyebrow.

"The mythical mermaid city made by the gods?"

"The very same."

"That no one has been able to locate and map since the first story was made about it?"

"Exactly."

Wolflock's sheer enthusiasm wavered for a moment under Mothy's scrutinising gaze, but his friend shrugged and flopped onto the floor next to him. "I'm in.

How are we doing this?"

"I'm glad you asked! We just need to-"

Wolflock stopped as Captain Blutro came back in, looking around and sniffed the air.

"Ah... I suspected as much. Boys, this room can't handle the mermaid any longer. Windows open or not. I won't be able to sleep with my sheets smelling like raw fish."

"But we're so close to finding the answers!" Wolflock pleaded.

The captain shook his head. "Take only the specific books you need and make your study base in the dining hall. Smartly, now."

They picked up the books Wolflock deemed that they needed, as well as a flora and fauna one with many pictures for Himi, and carted them back and forth to the dining hall. Mothy was in good spirits about the move because they could drink all the tea they wanted while they worked.

Himi followed them up and down, scooting along behind them like it was a game.

"I have to go and get my map and the captain's pencils. Keep her entertained for a moment, will you?" He waved at Mothy who nodded and started teaching Himi the common names for the creatures she pointed at.

He made his way back down the stairs, and he stopped outside Faleen and Bleen's door. Thick streams of incense smoke were wafting out and he could hear Faleen talking. It wasn't her usual haughty tone, but frightened and urgent. A sharp flash of satisfaction washed through him as he pressed his ear to the door.

The only noises he could make out were two people talking in what sounded like Northern Shellinmerth. He hadn't heard anyone on board speak any of the Shellinmerth languages. It had a distinct flow to it that made the sentences sound like one long word. Nothing like his own language, which gave clear separation to the words. Far more punctuated.

"What are you doing, Wolflock?"

He jumped in surprise and span mid-air to see Bleen behind him with her usual smile.

"Oh, nothing. Just... uh... resting. I'm still so weary from the accident last night."

"You poor thing. As long as you're not doing any investigating. We'll have to stop you for your own good, you know?" She wagged her long, manicured nail at him.

"Ha. Of course. Merry part," he nodded, turning on his heel and walking away as quickly as he could.

He felt her watching him as he made his way to the

Captain's cabin. He didn't want to let her know what he was up to, so he knocked and waited, leaning on the wall in the same way he'd done at her door.

Yes. This looks completely normal.

He picked at his nails, waiting for her to leave, when he saw Slavidus' door was ajar, hearing two voices starting to rise from the room. Bleen disappeared into her room and he ducked forward, peeking in.

Slavidus' room was perfectly straight and tidy in every way. His shoes were paired and lined up under his bed, his hairbrush sat perfectly aligned to his dresser and his shaving kit shone in the crescent moonlight as if they were on display in a high-end store. The only things that seemed untidy were a few of Yifi's items strewn about the place. One of her scarves hung from his mirror and a dress was draped over the back of his desk chair. Everything was also dust free.

But then his eyes caught on an unusually tangled, dusty mess of fishing poles and a harpoon in the corner between the arguing captain and first mate.

"I made them move into the dining hall with my antique books, Slavidus. They're not in the room next to you. What else do you want?"

"I want it gone! The moment he brought it back with him there's been nothing but trouble! The crew are miserable, the company is irritable, and I can't sleep."

"It's been half a day, man. I told them two nights. She saved his life. It's the minimum we could do. If I had it my way, we'd take her all the way to Creast, but I won't have you in this state for a week. Hours of it are bad enough."

"It'd find its way there anyway. I don't see the point in transporting it when nature should just take its course."

"You would sacrifice a child mermaid, an omen of good will from Aygir and Hatfjorn themselves? And one that is clearly as special as that one? You'd feed her to sharks and orcas and starvation?" the captain snarled. "I, for one, will not risk their wrath. Have we not had enough trouble on this voyage?"

"It's bad luck for it to be out of the water! What if the gods think we've stolen it?"

"She's not being forced to stay here. She knows she's safe and, as long as she is, so are we."

"But-"

"I won't hear another word on it. I've given the boys until Irid to find her pod's migration path. If they can't we'll hope to the sea that she's happy to travel with another ship to Creast Bay where she can rejoin them there."

"Blutro," Slavidus growled in a low tone, "if you

don't hold up to your word I'll go on strike."

Silence deafened the room.

"Two nights. This one is nearly over. Get some sleep and spend time with your lady. I need you fresh. You're not cursed, man. I won't let it happen a third time to you."

Wolflock leaped away from the door as Captain Blutro came out. He couldn't help but think of what an odd thing it was for the Captain to say as a parlay to Slavidus' demands.

"Mr Felen," he nodded with a tired roll of his eyes.

"Just getting my map, Captain."

"Very good. Believe you'll have any luck with your search?" He opened the door to his cabin for Wolflock.

"Who do you take me for? We don't need luck. We have scientific and mathematical deductions." He chuckled as he rolled up his map and grabbed the jar of pencils. "And a bunch of folklore tales riddled with glorified inaccuracies."

"Well," Blutro steered him out of the office and into the hallway as they made their way back to the deck, "if anyone can find math in folklore riddled with glorified inaccuracies, I would trust only you."

The captain made his way back to the helm in the light of the giant lanterns hung from the masts. Wolflock felt the ship lilt and his heart raced, thinking of what had happened to him the night before. He ran to the dining hall where a few people were milling about for supper. Just being within the walls of the hall made him feel safer, as well as Mothy's smiling face.

He wasn't smiling at Wolflock though. Nü had come into the kitchen to brew Parihaan's evening medicine and sterilise her pins.

"How goes the patient?" Wolflock asked, trying to hide his breathlessness from the dash.

"She stirred enough for me to test if she could feel sensations," Nü smiled with excitement. "She can feel her hands and thighs."

"Thighs? Not feet?"

Her smile dropped. "No. Not feet. I think she will be confined to a chair when she wakes. I am confident, now, that she will wake, though."

Wolflock looked to Himi, who watched them, with her giant pink eyes, keenly from the edge of the table where she rested her flubbery chin.

"Has Mothy officially introduced you?"

"Yes." She giggled like a bell. "She is much nicer than the mermaids back home. They are part demon or spirit and are vengeful. It is said they were born from the tears of injured women and will forever hate all people and animals."

"I love your stories. Even when they're scary," Mothy sighed, watching Nü with a dreamy stare.

"Demonology and magic are rather fascinating. I do believe that it should only be studied when practical though. Having a passing glance at it is sufficient until it becomes a key focus." Wolflock slowed his speech as he realised Himi was banging her tail in time with his syllables.

The others didn't have much to say to Wolflock's statement and fell silent, looking about the dining hall.

"You know I never noticed how much they used mermaids to decorate the ship with until today. I'm seeing them everywhere now," Mothy commented.

Wolflock followed his gaze to the wall where a large tapestry hung. It was obvious to him that mermaids were used all the way around the border. His eyes followed the tapestry down past the crown moulding to the dado rail. Everything on the ship had a level of flounce and swirl to it, but in doing that, much of the intricate craftsmanship was lost. It was perhaps one of the reasons Wolflock was just now seeing that the three defining strips of hand carved wood had various symbols on them. The floor had dolphins, the dado rail had hammerhead sharks, and the crown moulding had an intricate octopus.

"Hmm..." Wolflock frowned, getting up to pace along the wall as he ran his hand over it. "Curious."

Some of the sections had little blue stones and mirror shards in them. One of the mirror shards was even set into a tilted compass, moving with the ship. It wasn't pointing North though. It seemed to be fixed on a random point.

Broken. Maybe that's why it's being used as decoration.

He reached the kitchen storage area and realised the sacks of food stacked on barrels and crates was obscuring his vision of what he needed to see.

"What are you doing there, Wolflock?" He jumped, smelling the waft of incense that came off Bleen as she stood behind him.

"Argh! Oh. Nothing. I mean. I was just admiring the design."

"I meant about the library you've taken up the table with."

He blinked at the pile Nü and Mothy were now reading in comical voices to entertain Himi.

"It's Mothy's new study. He wants to learn about mermaids and Captain Blutro gave us everything he could find. I doubt he'll be able to get through it all. He's not as fast a reader as I am."

"I heard that!" Mothy laughed across the room, throwing a date at Wolflock's head.

Wolflock caught it and nodded to Bleen, hoping to part quickly, but she grabbed his arm.

"It's for your own good," she hissed through her smile. "You'll thank us one day. You should play everyone a song before bed. I haven't heard you play all day."

Wolflock frowned at her, yanking his arm free. "No. I only play when I want to. I'd appreciate you not nagging me any further."

Fury rose in his chest as he marched to the kitchen where Grogen was preparing the food for the breakfast shift in his lime trimmed apron. He looked out of the little stern facing window and leaned his arm on the rafter above him, scowling at the turbulent sea.

"May I have some tea, Grogen?" he sighed after a few tense minutes.

"Only if yeh say tha magic word, lad."

He heaved a heavier sigh and rolled his eyes. "Grogen is the best chef ever and no one can compare."

"I meant 'please', but that'll do. Tea comin' up."

Wolflock felt along the rafter and found the tiny slice the knife had left in it the night before when his rope had been cut. He wondered if, when he got to Mystentine University, they would let him hold experiments to see how different blades made various cuts on objects. Perhaps someone had already done the research and he just had to learn it.

He caught a glimpse of Bleen talking to Nü and Mothy, standing well clear of Himi. She didn't look like she was going to leave anytime soon, so he sat on the bench to talk to Grogen.

"You've been on the ship some time, Grogen. What do you know about the design?"

"The design?"

"More specifically, the design of this room and the hand carved animals on the walls."

"It's all carved from the grey wood from West Uluken. The whole ship is. Giant big trees tha' are like the sequoias from the East of Pyringel. Tha story goes tha' tha great, great, great, great, great grand pappy of Cap'in Blutro wanted to show his wife tha wonders o' the world, but she got terrible sick, so the only way he could do it was by boat. They sailed the ship all over Puinteyle. Eventually, his great, great, great gramma fell in love with tha whole Silver River after she inherited the ship fo' 'erself. She 'ad the whole thing refurbished with tha same grey wood and 'ad the big ol' wings installed on the sides so she could travel over tha ice. Said it was to catch them slippery varmints who kept stealing her jewels. Dunno what they meant by tha', but yeh know..."

Wolflock shrugged. He also had no idea "But when were the designs laid in?"

"Hmm... from my recollection that would 'ave been what 'is great, great pappy did when he started tradin' more with tha North and not chasin' varmints."

"Was this when he became obsessed with mermaids?"

Grogen scratched his beard, realised what he was doing, then rushed to wash his hands again before touching the benches. "Obsessed with mermaids? I don' know 'bout tha. But he 'ad a keen eye for wildlife, 'e did. Or so they say. I do know it was the great ship architect Franz Gudderwiest that did 'em, though. His signatures on everythin'. Was meant to be one of his crowning glories and whatnot. That's one of the biggest sellin' points for people comin' aboard, besides the ship ice skating."

"Franz Gudderwiest? He wasn't mentioned in any of the journals we've been looking at."

"Surely yeh've misread it somewhere. Him and the old, old, old Cap'in were brothers in law and he practically lived on the ship. 'E did his best work sailing as far away from his projects as he could."

"How do you know all of this, Grogen?"

The burly crewmate flushed tomato red, "I... I read. Things. Yeh know? I like a bit o' art as much as the next fella."

"I appreciate the information. Very enlightening." He glanced over to see Bleen hadn't left yet, even though Mothy and Nü both looked displeased.

"So... yeh got a reading yeh didn' like?"

"How'd you guess?" he muttered back darkly.

"Call it a hunch. If yeh want my advice, I'd tell yeh that you're the only one who makes yeh destiny. Yeh might make it harder or easier on yehself, but it's yours and yours alone. Don' let anyone tell yeh otherwise."

"I don't intend on it."

"Good. That's a good lad. Also..." He pushed a tiny key into Wolflock's hand from the kitchen drawer. "That's the little entranceway cupboard key. That'll keep Mothy's research books safe if 'e doesn' want anyone spoiling his studies."

Wolflock smirked. "Thanks, Grogen." Bleen finally departed with a final attempt at a warm stare in his direction. "Well, thanks for the tea. I'd best help Mothy with his studies, or else he'll never learn enough to get this mermaid home."

CHAPTER 7
Fishing for Clues

Wolflock made his way back to the dining table and unfurled his mess of a map. Had he not drawn it himself, it would have taken him hours to make any sense of it. Nü and Mothy stared in wonder.

"I see you're not artistically inclined?" Mothy snorted, rolling the corner.

"You've seen my shoe sketches. You know I can draw."

"What is this then? It looks like a dog's breakfast?"

"What?"

"It does look like a child has made drawings on a

map," Nü said tracing her nail along one of the lines the dolphins followed. "I think it is called 'abstract'?"

"These are the migration patterns on the dolphins and possibly mermaids, as well as the ship's navigation over the last hundred years. And here we have the currents and spotted volcanic vents." He was too pleased with the success of his research to be snappy with them. "Ninety years ago, the captain's great, great grandfather reported seeing mermaids here. Then nine years prior and post, here and here. We need to find when the first time the mermaids were recorded being sighted by the Silver Ice Hair was and the last time his great, great grandfather saw them. The first should be dated one hundred and eight or one hundred and seventeen years ago, thereabouts, and the last sighting should be around eighty-one or seventy-two years ago."

"Why those years?"

"My theory is that the mermaids appear on a nine-year cycle in the areas the Silver Ice Hair navigates. That means that we are on one of those cycles this very year. The evidence shows a very conclusive pattern, even if the previous captains were unaware of it. There has also been mention of dolphins, sharks, and octopuses in several instances, so, somehow, those have relevance too. If we can measure the distance by the swimming speed of the mermaids between where we have seen them and Creast, we may be able to determine by simple math where Sinalta is."

"Yes. Of course. Simple math. Anyone could do it," Mothy chuckled.

"If it is not measuring herbs or reductions in symptoms, you will have to excuse me. I will cover your watch for Parihaan this night." Nü stood up and nodded to them both.

"Would you do tomorrow night, too?" Wolflock asked, not looking up from the journal he was checking.

Her silence made him look up. She stared at him with a flat expression.

"Please?"

"No. You must offer me a better thing than please. Friends don't say please in Xiayah."

"Uhh... what do you want, then?"

Without any hesitation she said, "You will give up a whole night and day vigil for me when this is finished."

"That sounds fair. We can do that."

"Oh no," she teased. "Only you, Wolflock. I am only covering your watch."

"Fine. I hereby swear that you shall have one night and one day's vigil from me when deemed necessary."

"Very good. Write it down and I will collect the

promise as payment after tomorrow night."

She departed with her head high and Wolflock returned to his search through the books as Mothy snickered. Glaring at his friend in reproach, he realised Himi wasn't in sight. He peeked over the edge of the table to find her sleeping on the floor, using one of the navigation books as a pillow.

The night drew on and on; Wolflock realised that key entries were missing from the journals.

"If I read one more log about emergency potatoes, I'm going to throw this across the room," Wolflock snarled, waving one of the faded blue books. Mothy half laughed and set aside his stack of five brown journals.

"Not a hair nor hide... nor scale, of a mermaid mentioned in these ones. Have you already finished all twenty of those?"

"Twenty-eight."

"No way!" Mothy leaned forward and touched the spine of each one as he counted. "You must be tired. There are only twenty-six."

"I beg your pardon, my friend, but I remember distinctly seeing twenty-eight in the Captain's study."

"Check for yourself then, but there are only twenty-six."

Wolflock frowned and patronisingly counted each

one. "Twenty-five. Twenty-six, twenty... wait, what?"

There were, indeed, only twenty-six.

"Did we leave them in the Captain's study?"

Wolflock knew they didn't. The last thing he had collected from the Captain's study was the map. Someone else had heard what they were doing in the Captain's study, though. Someone who had demanded that the Captain make them move.

"Keep an eye on Himi. I'll be back."

He snatched up two of the blue faded journals and dashed out of the room without another word, slipping and sliding across the deck to the entrance to the cabins. It was shut. He'd never seen it shut before. He didn't even know it could shut.

He slid his hands around where the entrance should be and felt a heavy silver ring. With all his strength as the rain poured on his back, he heaved the door until it slid open enough to scurry inside. Wolflock wiped his wet black hair out of his face and charged to the First Mate's room. The books had to be in there.

He could smell the thick, sickly sweet smell of incense smoke seeping out from under the twin's door and made a face. The company were tucked away in their rooms, occasionally meandering to their neighbours when they grew bored. The hallway lanterns were dimmed, though, making it difficult to see anyone too far down the hall without specifically looking for them.

Using this darkness, Wolflock silently opened the door to Slavidus' room. He peeked in, expecting to see the First Mate sleeping, but nothing. No one was present. Was he getting his reading done? Yifi wasn't in here either. Were they getting it done together?

Not wanting to lose any time, Wolflock slipped into the neat cabin.

"If I were a fastidious first mate, where would I hide the journals that I didn't want an appraising investigator to find?" he muttered to himself, going through the bedside table and desk.

Only two things seemed out of place. His bed was only half made. The side Slavidus slept on was peeled back and the pillow on Yifi's side was turned vertically along the bed with a pole thrown across it. Wolflock knew Slavidus was observant. He had noticed when his shoes had been bumped when the young investigator had rushed under his bed, so he didn't dare touch the bed. He did notice that two smears of what looked like red blood had been smeared towards Slavidus' side. No more than a shaving nick.

Wolflock turned his attention to the fishing poles tangled in their cylindrical holder crammed in the corner.

They were furthest from the bed and out of view of the sleeper, but not someone at the desk.

"Hmm... a place of contemplation and distraction... but not wanting to induce nightmares? He doesn't want to look at it while he sleeps, but he hasn't disposed of it. He wants the reminder still... curious."

Knowing Slavidus, Wolflock deduced that he would feel guilty about taking the Captain's property. He was an honest and honourable man, as well as the hardest working person on the ship. The dishevelled fishing kit was where he would stow away objects he felt bad for taking. He put his hand down into the container, feeling around for anything book shaped.

"Ouch!"

Wolflock yanked his hand free of a hook that had caught his middle finger. He sucked the injury as it bled, glaring at the treacherous equipment. In the faded light of the room his eyes widened. Now that he looked at the fishing poles and tangled line, he could see a dark yellow dried substance on them. Two of the fishing rods had lines covered in what looked like dried blood, except that it was a yellowy orange. It was so old that it flaked off when he touched it, leaving a stain on the fine cord.

No book though. Surely, I'm not wrong on this.

He dug down in the container with his right hand

this time, being far more cautious. There wasn't any book, but his fingers grazed something that felt like paper. He pinched the corner with his index and middle finger, drawing it out and plucking the persistent hook from it.

It was a small palm sized piece of paper that looked like the same paper as the faded blue journals. Had this hook caught onto the book as someone pulled it from the container?

Wolflock looked over it, certain it had been torn from the journal, and even more convinced when he saw the same handwriting on both sides of it. The words were something about seeing beauty and delivering fruit for them to play with. What was beauty and who was playing with the fruit could only be speculation, but he knew that Slavidus had the journals. He just needed to know where they were now.

Slavidus was getting a reading. Possibly about the journals themselves. He slipped out of Slavidus' room and made his way to the twin's door, making a face at the smoke seeping out from the edges. He noted that it had a slightly purple tinge to it and left a light dusting of purple residue as it settled. If he could just pick Slavidus' pocket, he'd be able to get the journals and replace them with the ones he'd already read through.

The longer he stood outside the door, the hazier his mind got. The muffled chatter inside the room grew slower and softer, and the stench of the smoke made him woozy. He stepped away and, instantly, his mind began to clear. There was something wrong with the smoke.

He drew his handkerchief and wiped the ground, examining the sample. It had a similar purple colour to the herbs on the cloth he'd found weeks ago when everyone had gotten sick from the river bugs in the stew.

"Interesting..." he muttered to himself.

A moment later the door opened and Yifi rushed out, barging passed him and slamming the door to her own room. Wolflock could have sworn she saw tears in her eyes. Slavidus rushed out behind her, but Wolflock stepped out. In the second he had to observe, he saw Slavidus had the journals in his hand. The pair collided and Wolflock made a deliberate movement to knock the books to the ground.

"Goodness! I'm so sorry Slavidus. I got all turned about. Here, let me get those for you." He scooped the books off the ground and shuffled them, putting the two he wanted behind his back.

"Wolflock! What are you doing? Why are you up so late?"

"Mothy and I are sleeping in the dining hall. I just

came to get something to mask the odour and forgot myself when I breathed in the smoke in the hallway."

"Breathed in the smoke?"

"Oh yes. The incense smoke the twins use is much too thick and strong. It seems to dizzy my faculties."

"Wolflock," Bleen cooed as she poked her head out of the door, "won't you come in, sweetie?"

He screwed his face up involuntarily and shook his head, revolted at the pet name.

"No. Merry part, Slavidus."

The first mate raised an eyebrow in confusion, holding the books closer to his chest at Wolflock's lack of propriety with the purpled haired psychic. "Uh... Merry part. Stay safe."

"Close the hatch behind me." And with that Wolflock was back on the open deck, in the rain, with his missing journals.

Upon his return to the dining hall, he was met with a horrendous shrieking of the violin and mermaid.

"What in the name of Aygir are you doing?" Wolflock shoved his fingers in his ears until Mothy stopped.

"You made it look so easy and Himi was crying for you."

"It didn't sound like playing for her made her

stop," he laughed as he took the instrument from his friend.

"She was getting restless, and I just wanted to cheer her up. I tried getting her to point at the map where her home is, but I don't think she can read maps."

Wolflock plucked at the strings to bring the violin back into tune, feeling something echo in the back of his mind. "It is believed that they can navigate, though." The notes came back on key quickly. "That's interesting. Their big eyes might mean they are nocturnal. They may navigate by the stars. That's why they aren't on the major currents like the dolphins. Anyway, I have to read through these two journals because I suspect they'll tell us the true significance of the mermaid iconography around the ship."

"Are you thinking the Captain's great, great grandpa found Sinalta?"

"Oh, I don't think. I know. His notes are the first key to finding Himi's home."

"Key? Is there a lock?"

"Give me a few minutes and I'll find out."

"And what do I do in the meantime?"

Wolflock looked up blinking. "Huh?"

"How can I help? I can't let you do it all yourself. We might not get Himi home in time."

"Oh. Umm... We need to draw a new map for us to plot where Sinalta is and how long it will take us to get there. Then use my notes to draw the Silver Ice Hair's route."

"On it!"

Mothy moved excitedly as he began drawing the Hatfjorn Sea map on the tablecloth, shoving the books to the edges as he drew. Wolflock buried his nose in the journal with the earliest dates.

Sidumpus the 9th of Nibit'ling Ickst in the thirty-sixth year of the reign of Queen Ni'ia the Fifth

I cannot believe it. My first day as the unofficial Captain of the Silver Ice Hair. Mother is sick and can't man the helm. The doctor thinks she'll be sick until Creast. She said she was going to give me captaincy when we returned to Shellinden, but this has given me the reins early. I was so frightened, but we had the best possible omen ever. We saw dolphins. This is going to be a great voyage.

Sollempus the 12th of Nibit'ling Ickst in the thirty-sixth year of the reign of Queen Ni'ia the Fifth

The weather is fair and mother's metal wings have been a new thing to learn, but they're going strong. One of the new crew got a bit spooked when he saw a great hammerhead shark just before we hit the ice. We're making good time.

Lucimpus the 15th of Nibit'ling Ickst in the thirty-sixth year of the reign of Queen Ni'ia the Fifth

Mother has recovered enough to come out and see the octopus that attached to the side of the ship, but she doesn't want to take over again. I think she wants to retire.

Relimpus the 21st of Nibit'ling Ickst in the thirty-sixth year of the reign of Queen Ni'ia the Fifth

The best blessing to ever come upon the ship has found us. We sailed past the blue city of Sinalta. Such tall towers. Such majesty. The mermaids played with the crew in the lifeboat. They gave them each a pretty blue stone and then gave mother nine. The mermaids have such magic when they sing. Mother is going to help me lay them out so we can find our way back again.

Sidumpus the 9th of Nibit'ling Ickst in the thirty-

seventh year of the reign of Queen Ni'ia the Fifth

We brought the dolphins. A good song from us all helps. I'm making sure the crew storage is stocked with all the best instruments and song books. The dolphins followed us well along the way to Irid. There is no frost, though. Perhaps that is why we couldn't find our way back through.

Lucimpus the 8th of Nibit'ling Ickst in the thirty-eighth year of the reign of Queen Ni'ia the Fifth

Dolphins again this year and music makes the morale of the ship high, so the crew don't mind the detour. No sight of Sinalta though.

Culimpus the 11th of Nibit'ling Ickst in the thirty-sixth year of the reign of Queen Ni'ia the Fifth

We are off the currents, and we saw no signs.

The old captain went nine years and through the death of his mother before he had any luck sighting the mermaids again. His entries grew despondent and, after twenty-seven years of diligent searching, he started believing it had all been a dream. Wolflock then moved to the notes in the last journey, searching for the important parts.

Sidumpus the 9th of Nibit'ling Ickst in the sixty-third year of the reign of Queen Ni'ia the Fifth

The crew said they played for the dolphins today. I'm glad they're happy. We must hasten to Irid as Mrs Vrecus is due to give birth any day now and our only midwife has minimal experience.

Sollempus the 12th of Nibit'ling Ickst in the sixty-third year of the reign of Queen Ni'ia the Fifth

Bracus said he saw a shark today as it stole his fish. Everyone else has put him in a foul mood by not believing his story. I dreamed of mother. She was singing to the stones. I checked that they were all in place. All secure. For the first time, I noticed mirrors placed in certain areas. I am curious as to what they're for.

Lucimpus the 15th of Nibit'ling Ickst in the sixty-third year of the reign of Queen Ni'ia the Fifth

I'm furious. I had to stop the lads from spearing an octopus that climbed on board. Poor thing didn't know where it was. It was huge though. Its arms were as long as I am tall. I sent it off with a fish. Bloody thing was strong. No sweets for the boys. Thank goodness the lasses in the crew saw sense to come get me. I am curious, though. But I won't hope. We have a job to do.

Relimpus the 21st of Nibit'ling Ickst in the sixty-third year of the reign of Queen Ni'ia the Fifth

What a day! What a day. We stopped the ship to see mermaids that swam around and around us. We lowered the lifeboats to get a better look. Mrs Vrecus was in the early stages of labour but insisted on going down. I never thought I'd see them again. We couldn't move as she started giving birth in earnest right in the lifeboat! The mermaids were so fascinated, watching with their big black eyes. They brought her tough weed to clench in her jaw and splashed her hair with cool water while Brohdie acted as midwife. She had a healthy baby girl and one of the mermaids gave her a little blue stone as a gift and sang. Our ship is still blessed. The cook said the kitchen lit up with a beautiful blue light when they sang, but it faded quickly. I think I can pass the ship on to my son, happy now I've seen them just once more.

Wolflock set the diary down and looked around the room. Mothy had finished his map and the few channels he could make sense of. He had been so engrossed in reading that he hadn't noticed Mothy pull over sacks from the storage and fashioned them into a nest. He also hadn't noticed how sleep had tried to push its way into his eyes. He locked the documents and books away in the cupboard Grogen had given him the key to, pocketing the key before he assessed the sleeping situation.

He had to keep an eye on Himi, and he wasn't about to leave Mothy to sleep alone on the floor. Well, he wasn't really alone. Himi was sleeping cuddled up with a bag of almond meal. Wolflock unlaced a few of the seat cushions and laid a clean tea towel across it. The only time he'd slept on the floor was when he made sure no one could get into Parihaan's room. He laid a tablecloth across Mothy and curled up amongst the pile of sacks and pillows.

Himi opened her pink eyes a sliver and hummed. As Wolflock gave her a small wave and closed his eyes, he drifted to sleep to the sound of her humming. He floated into an odd sleep, hearing the echoing song, and seeing a faint aqua glow as if he were sinking under the blue waves of the sea.

CHAPTER 8

The Curse of Intellect

*Y*ou *can't wake up to a smell, Wolflock!" Myna snapped at him.*

"Then why did your stupid experiment wake me up? I can smell the failed perfume from down the hall. Stop using seal fat! It's suffocating!"

"Oh, that's not the smell that's suffocating you." His sister took off her lab coat and sealed the tiny bottle of perfume she'd wasted two buckets of roses on.

Wolflock felt as if he were trying to carry a house on his back and he couldn't draw a deep breath.

"That's the mermaid you've been carrying."

Wolflock's eyes snapped open out of the dream and he coughed. Himi's heavy form sat on his chest and stomach as she braided the longer bits of his hair.

"Off! Please!" he gasped, pinching her through her thick hide.

She rolled off him, making that throaty laugh she did when she was entertained, slapping the floor. He spluttered and wheezed in the grey morning light, heaving his chest to catch his breath. He watched her bounce on her chubby tummy to the stacked storage area next to the kitchen, where Mothy had dragged their bedding from. Before he could stop her, she hoisted herself onto the first crate and tore down a second large crate. It crashed and shattered on the ground, scattering dried snacks all over the floor.

Mothy threw his arms and legs out, smacking Wolflock in the face. He fell backwards with a thump into the sacks, just as Himi chased after the snacks, toppling more containers on her way down.

"Wolflock?" Mothy blinked, still not quite awake.

"Himi!" Wolflock scowled, holding what felt like a bloody nose.

"Urf, urf!"

"Wolflock!" Matroos burst into the dining hall.

Wolflock exhaled, pinching the bridge of his nose.

Himi began scoffing the dried snacks while Matroos failed to shoo her away, and Mothy looked on as if he were still dreaming.

"Look at this mess! My kitchen smells like fish! Get her out of here."

"Himi, come on. You can eat what you can carry."

"You get started on... whatever we are doing today," Mothy waved Wolflock away. "I'll help clean this up."

Wolflock helped him to his feet and gave his shoulder a grateful pat, "Thank you, Mothy. Join us when you're done."

Wolflock only had time to pull out their map and case of pencils before hastening out of the dining hall with Himi. He had to admit that the air was far fresher out on the open deck. He stretched his back, arms, and legs, smoothing his hair back, catching his fingers on the braid Himi had made for him. She looked up at him with her big pink eyes, stuffing the last of the snacks into her mouth.

"You look like a child. I hope that food doesn't make you sick. Let's speak with the Captain and see what he thinks of our map."

They made their way up to the helm platform, Wolflock still wiping the sleep from his eyes.

"Merry morning, Captain," he yawned.

"Big night, lad?"

"You could say that. And an early start. Someone was hungry. And bored." He untangled the braid.

"I can't imagine what that's like. Having someone disturb your peace because they're bored. How awful."

"I know you can't mean me," he snorted. "I'll tell you now, Captain, it puts one off having pets."

"How goes the search for her pod?"

"I want to talk to you about that. See," he knelt down and unrolled the map, "we have been able to locate a general area we can expect to see her pod. It is slightly off course, but it shouldn't delay us by more than a day."

Captain Blutro's face creased with a frown, "That is a mighty big area, Wolflock. We can only be delayed by half a day. You'll have to narrow down your search further. These broad searches tend to draw matters out more than they ought. You've got another night though, so I'm sure you can find them. Who knows, we may still spot them from the crow's nest. Good work on the currents, though. They're different from the textbooks I remember, but I feel like our current route follows yours more closely."

"Yes," Wolflock rolled the map back up, "they do."

Without another word he sat on the steps with Himi, thinking about how he could possibly narrow down his search. He'd collected all the research and data he could from the information on the ship. Was there something he'd missed?

Himi tried to braid his hair again but he swatted her away, glaring at the horizon with his tired eyes. She grew bored and rolled down the stairs, sniffing things around the deck and chewing on the edges of different objects.

He knew there was a significance between finding mermaids and the appearance of dolphins, hammerhead sharks and octopuses. The words 'heart' and 'song' kept recurring, and the city of Sinalta never seemed to be in the same place. Were there multiple giant crystal blue cities? But then, how did they return to the same place to find it empty?

As Wolflock stared out, it took him a moment to realise someone was waving at him. Bleen scooted passed Himi, who peeled her lips back in a snarl, and sat on the stairs next to Wolflock.

"Merry meet and good morning, my musical friend. How goes your fish-sitting?" She giggled at her own pun.

"Himi is a mammal. Not a fish." Wolflock leaned

his cheek into his hand, trying to bring his thoughts back to any clues he'd missed.

"I was awake early to clear my mind and get a cup of tea, but the dining hall smells awful, so I came out here and..."

The thick smell of incense smoke flooded around him and his mind turned hazy, but instead of becoming confused, he just sank deeper into his thoughts. He could see that her deep purple lipstick had a glossy sheen to it and when she spoke, he could smell a strong scent of peppermint. He tuned out her words, watching as Himi arched back to look at the sky. She did this movement over and over, as if she were searching for something. There were no clouds today, and no birds.

What is she looking for?

"Captain, I'm not swapping with you until she's out of sight."

Wolflock's attention was jerked back by Slavidus complaining. He stood next to the stairs to the helm, pressing himself as far away from Himi as he could get.

"She's not causing any harm, man. She stinks too bad to put her indoors."

"...And, so, I was hoping that you would play for us over breakfast as it would lift all our spirits and maybe even-"

"Just put her over into the water, then, if she's being such an issue!"

The captain put a knuckle to his temple, "Slavidus, I said-"

"I'll take Himi around the back." Wolflock stood up quickly, bored of the irritating conversations going on around him. "You won't see her, Slavidus."

He yawned again as he moved down the stairs, his mind clearing the second he got close to Himi. With a sharp frown, he looked back at Bleen, whose welcoming demeanour looked menacing now that he had full view of her. Her knuckles were white from balling her fists and the muscles in her jaw extended out from how tightly she was clenching her teeth.

Slavidus didn't look much happier, gripping the spokes on the wheel as if he were going to snap them off. With a sigh and a shake of his head, Wolflock summoned Himi to follow him and they left the tense centre deck.

"Is that you Lockie?" Mothy called from the window as they came around.

"Aye. Himi and I are trying to stay out of everyone's way back here. How is your cleaning going?"

"Oh, you know. Not bad." A dried piece of fish jerky flew out of the window, catching Himi's attention.

"The smell has nearly gone and I'm just looking for any bits I may have missed." Another piece of jerky soared out. Himi leaped up and caught it in her mouth, making Wolflock chuckle. "I don't think Himi will like the breakfast Matroos has prepared, so I'm going to make her a special fish cake and see if she likes it." He flung another treat through the window. Himi missed this time and it flicked off her nose.

"You're not a good shot with those, you know?" Wolflock snorted, unrolling the map again to work on.

"You try and hit things you can't see and tell me you're any better."

Wolflock shrugged and began pacing with the map held out in front of him.

"Be careful," came a husky gruff voice.

"Huh? Oh. Merry meet, Hognut."

The hairy crewmate nodded, tapping out his pipe over the side of the ship while Himi continued her back stretches.

"What in Hatfjorn's name are yeh doin'?"

"Trying to find the mythical city of Sinalta and help Himi get home."

"O' course yah are..." he sighed, packing his pipe with fresh smoke. After a few moments. where Wolflock expected him to walk away, Hognut gestured for the map.

"Well give us a look, then."

Surprised, Wolflock passed the map over. It was the most sociable he'd ever seen Hognut in his months on the ship.

"Oi. See this. That's wrong. There's an island there tha' the seals have babies. Won't be there. And tha'. Won't be there."

"Why not?" Wolflock asked as he passed the bearded man a pencil.

"Cause that's too hot. Sometimes yah see the fire under the water when it's sunny and clear."

"You mean volcanoes?"

Hognut looked at him with his beady little black eyes through his shaggy rusty hair. "Yeah."

"Where do you think it is?"

"Dunno. We travel over these areas nearly every year though, so not in these ones either."

"How can you be sure?"

Hognut lit his pipe, making Wolflock catch the pencil as it tried to roll away. He took a few short puffs then a deep exhale before he spoke again. "I remember every place I ever ash my pipe.'

His gruff tone was so resolute that Wolflock couldn't argue.

"Why're yah tryin' ta navigate by map anyway? Yah

better off going by stars. If I had to put deimas on it, I'd say Sinalta is always under the mermaid's heart."

"What do you mean?"

"It's a star at the centre of the mermaid constellation. Every year the mermaid sits over the sea and every nine years her heart beats. It's a big blue star. Only comes out for a little bit, though."

"How long is a little bit?"

"Dunno."

"Would you happen to know where the stars sit on my map? I can't say I'm much of an astronomer."

"Dunno what tha' is. Stars move, lad. Yah see 'em move across the sky every night. Just wait for tonight and see. Don't do anymore of this thinkin' work today. Yah already stirrin' too much trouble for yahself."

"It's not like you to be worried. What trouble have you heard?"

Hognut took another deep breath on his pipe. "Them twins say yah cursed when yah use yah brain. Got the crew in a tizzy tellin' em the s'morning tha' mermaids out of water is bad luck." He looked over at Himi, who was reaching for more snacks to come out of the window. "She's just a creature. Might be magic. Might not. The crew are gettin' antsy, though."

Wolflock sighed through his nose. "Thanks for the

forewarning. We'll try and stay out of sight until tonight. Will you show me the constellation to look for? Perhaps I can convince the Captain to veer in that direction."

With his pipe hanging out of the side of his beard, Hognut drew a set of eight asterixis in an uneven pattern. He joined them with lines and Wolflock could just make out how they could resemble a mermaid.

"The heart is meant to appear somewhere here. Now, keep yah nose outta trouble til yah see em and most everyone else has gone ta bed."

"You have been surprisingly helpful, Hognut. Thank you kindly."

"Thanks Hognut," Mothy called timidly from the kitchen.

With a grunt and a nod, he left to return to his duties. Wolflock pocketed the map and leaned on the back rail with a smile.

"Did you hear that, Mothy? We'll be able to get Himi home tonight."

"Yep."

Something about his soft tone told Wolflock he didn't share his enthusiasm.

"Are you well?"

"Yep."

"Well clearly not. What's happened? Did you

hear something I didn't... because I sincerely doubt it!" Wolflock climbed onto the crate under the window and peeked in, seeing the top of Mothy's straw blond head.

"It's been cloudy every night. We haven't been able to see the stars."

"We have a hypothetical location. It's worth a try."

"I suppose..." His shoulders raised around his ears as he dusted off the jerky snacks.

"What is really upsetting you?"

Mothy stopped, taking a slow inhale before he spoke again. It was clear he was choosing his words carefully.

"Do you think you're cursed?"

Wolflock blinked. "What?"

"I'm just worried, is all. What if something bad happens like the twins said?"

His mouth flattened in distaste at the topic. "I don't think I'm cursed, but, if it will help, I recently found out Yifi's mother was a genuine witch. I'll go and ask her for an amulet or a charm, or something to ward it off until we get Himi home. Then I promise not to get into anymore investigative trouble until you agree to join me. Would that help?"

"As long as it works. Yes. Thank you, Lockie. I was worried I'd have to hide away to stay safe."

"Why would you think that?"

"Because," Mothy averted his grey blue eyes, "they told me if I... I had to be careful around harpoons. I've been nervous about what could be interpreted as a harpoon ever since."

"Would you like me to see if Yifi will make you an anti-bad-fortune-telling-charm too?"

"Get out of here," Mothy chuckled, throwing a snack at Wolflock's head as he ducked out of the way.

"Keep Himi entertained until I get back," he called over his shoulder and descended into the open cabin deck.

Wolflock tapped on Yifi's doorframe as the door was open. She sat at her dresser, holding her large citrine pendant, and stared intently at her face as it morphed. Her eyebrows rounded, thickened then thinned. Her cheekbones flared and withdrew, and her chestnut hair changed from sleek and vibrant, to a little frizzy with grey threads.

"Sorry to interrupt," he spoke up, stepping inside before she gave permission. He needed to get this task done so he could back to helping Himi.

Yifi's appearance returned to the pretty but average one she'd chosen the night she first got the pendant and she turned on her stool to face him. "Wolflock?"

"I didn't know that was how your pendant worked. Can you change your appearance at will?"

She smiled, her lips a touch drier and thinner than when they had first met. "I think it may take some mastery, but it's a nice enchantment. Just subtle. You can't change your overall skin colour, hair colour or shape. I think, with practice, I may be able to add impressive bags under my eyes and say I'm too tired for social events. I have been able to change my eye colour from black tea to oak though."

"That is so fascinating. Father never let my sister or I use any magic or enchanted objects in the house. He said it would make us lazy and reliant. Little did he realise that we would just use chemistry and contraptions to become lazy and reliant on."

Yifi giggled, gesturing to her desk chair for him to use. "What brings you to me?"

"Hognut told us that the twins have been telling people I'm cursed when I investigate things. Apparently, research counts as investigating. They're getting-"

"Upset?"

"Troublesome."

"Ah." She nodded thoughtfully. "Do you need a shoulder? Someone to talk to?"

"Oh no. Nothing like that. Mothy feels

uncomfortable and I thought you might know a charm or anti curse procedure?"

"Do you think you're cursed?"

"Definitely not," Wolflock said. "Nothing abnormal has happened and I do wish Mothy would be a bit more rational, but we have to get Himi home before morning."

"Being swept off the ship into freezing waters is normal for you?"

"I was saved by a mermaid. I feel like the events evened out."

"Have you encountered any other trouble while investigating?"

Wolflock frowned. Was she trying to convince him that he was cursed? "I mean, I had a terrible night sleep because we had to keep an eye on Himi, and she's not allowed in small, enclosed places due to her odour. Slavidus has been obtrusive and Bleen has been intrusive."

"That is all external. Rudimentary curses that induce bad luck or poor feelings to the person or object look like that. Mother would use them on my competition to any Beltaine balls. How have you been feeling, though?"

Realising she wasn't accusing him of being cursed,

but, rather, probing for the root problem, he relaxed. "Ever since my reading with the twins, I have felt off. I felt hazy, like I was too stupid to think for myself. I actually thought I should look for a way to be a musician like they told me to. I thought I had to give up being an appraising investigator, even though it felt so right when Mothy and I spoke earlier. Bleen keeps nagging me to play the violin. I..." he sighed, leaning forward with his elbows on his knees, "I'm exhausted. Like I'm fighting fate in the dark. If I never picked up that stupid violin maybe my reading would have been different."

"Yes. It would have."

Wolflock looked up, his eyebrows deeply creased.

"You're not cursed. You're suffering from opinionated advice."

His shoulders slumped, releasing the tension he wasn't aware he was holding on to.

"For some reason, I don't know why, they gave you a reading with something they wanted to tell you in mind. Instead of just saying it, they were too cowardly and used the cards as a shield. You didn't get a reading. You were given an opinion. My mother would do the same thing when the ladies she thought were my competition would come to see which suitors they should pursue and ignore. She'd tell them to avoid the men she wanted to line up for me. There may have been kernels of truth in what she told them, but they were so highlighted that it changed the entire reading. It also made them feel like they had no free will in their fate.”

“No free will?”

“Wolflock,” Yifi smiled, the corners of her eyes creasing warmly, “the future is always fluid. Even the most precise palmistry, cards and scientific reports combined can never be fully accurate. If any one of the women my mother turned away from their suitors had instead thought to work on the problems their relationships could suffer, perhaps they would have had a fulfilling partnership. If you have been told your investigating will put you in danger, you have three choices. Possibly more, but three I see.”

“Huh?” Wolflock tilted his head as she phrased her sentence peculiarly.

“Sorry. Giving readings has a level of theatrics. Knowing your future means you can accept it, fight it, or prepare for it. That is your choice. Anyone that tells you otherwise is a fool or cruel.”

Her last words came out with a hiss of venom he hadn’t heard from her before. “Did the twins tell Slavidus something that drove a wedge between you?”

“I shouldn’t be surprised, but how did you know

that?"

"You haven't been sleeping in his room, you both looked upset last night when he received his reading about the journals and mermaids, and you're playing with your appearance, which you only do when you're upset. It's a self-soothing action and seems to have become even more so since your appearance isn't stagnant."

"I told him not to get a reading," she sighed. "They told him to not trust those closest to him because they didn't know the truth. Some truth. I think they're simply scared that the magic of a single mermaid is stronger than anything they can imagine having. I didn't want to sleep in his bed when he's been cradling that stupid harpoon. I swear, he thinks some giant, deep-sea creature, or the gods themselves, are going to rise up and destroy the ship."

Wolflock chuckled. Yifi's attitude was refreshing and brought him immense comfort from knowing his future was his choice.

"Now. About Mothy. Do you still have your magnifying glass?"

He smirked and drew it from his pocket. "Ah yes. My very special gift from you. Rosewood handle and gold painted rim. A gift showing true love and a desire for my eyes to rest as I read the copies letters you're going to send me."

Yifi snatched it off him and screwed up her nose. "Just be thankful I passed it forward to you and didn't throw it away."

"That would have been a great waste."

She lit a white candle and dripped it on the handle of the magnifying glass, then pressed her sealing stamp onto it, curling it around the handle to leave a clear mark.

"It's not much, but it looks fancy. I always seal my letter with this sigil to prevent them being opened by those that shouldn't read them. On your now sacred talisman, no one will be able to magically interfere with the luck of your affairs."

"I was just hoping for a couple of scratches and a quick chant to say to convince Mothy."

"Do you want to be prepared for your dangerous fate or not?"

"I mean... yes. But will this work?"

She passed him the magnifying glass with the now dry thick wax seal. "What do you think? In your search, if you can find anything that may help Slavidus overcome his fear of mermaids, I would appreciate it."

Wolflock shrugged. "I'll keep my eyes open for you." He nodded his thanks and stepped out of her room.

For the first time in two days, he couldn't smell the thick incense leaking out of the twin's room. He drew a deep breath and took half a step towards the upper deck before he turned on his heel and marched towards Slavidus room. While he had chatted to Yifi, everyone had moved to breakfast and Slavidus was at the helm. His room would be free to check for more information, and perhaps to plant something to allay his anxiety. It was the least he could do for Yifi helping him with Mothy.

As he passed the entrance to the crew quarters, Grogen bumped into him, his arms stacked with picnic blankets and tent poles.

"Sorry lad! S'cuse me."

"What are you entertaining us with today, Grogen?" Wolflock smiled and pushed one of the poles into a more secure crook of his arm.

"We will be conducting a blessing for the ship," Faleen said as she came up after Grogen, her arms also filled with tent poles, the canopy, and a basket dangling from her arm. "Our fellow travellers will be more comfortable out of the weather. We would love your musical accompaniment. It will add power to the blessing for our safe travels."

"Oh?" Wolflock screwed up his face, glancing around for a way to end the conversation without them being suspicious. "Yes. Let me get my things. I'm sure Parihaan could do with some of that blessing magic to speed her recovery."

Faleen looked at him with her flat, irritated expression. "Blessings work better when the collective follows a single purpose."

"Of course. How silly of me to wish for a more difficult situation to become simpler, rather than something I am confident in others' abilities to perform."

Grogen shrugged and moved on to the upper deck, unable to comprehend Wolflock's meaning, but knowing he was being rude. He could tell Faleen wanted to stay and fight him, but she was carrying the poles with metal joins, making them heavier than the one's Grogen took. Her endurance couldn't stand up to Wolflock's smug grin and she had to move along or drop her items. She chose to move along, shuffling the basket filled with incense, crystals and three bottles of red ointment. He turned and watched her leave, grinning with utmost satisfaction.

A door closed behind him. "Did I hear that correctly? You're going to play for our blessing?"

All sense of accomplishment left him as the thick smell of incense and peppermint stung his nostrils. "Yes. I have agreed to it."

Bleen clicked her talon-like nails together in excitement. "How positively charming! It's so wonderful to see you embracing your destiny. This is going to be the start of wonderful things! Faleen has told me so much."

"Yes, well, I'm sure. I must get my things. I'll... be up as soon as I can be. There's some sheet music in the storage room I need."

"I can't wait!" She squealed and pulled at his clothes to straighten them. He rolled his eyes, but when she persisted for too long, he swatted her hands and she walked off with a high giggle.

As she left, he realised that the smell of the incense hadn't made him hazy. Perhaps Yifi's charm did work. He waited for Bleen to be out of sight before he slipped into Slavidus' room again.

He felt as if he was getting rather familiar with the first mate's space. The bed was still dishevelled on one side, but there was no pole across the pillow. Had that been the harpoon Yifi had mentioned? It would explain the blood if it were sharp. It wasn't in the fishing pole container, either.

The only other change in the room was that the desk had an open book and striped sachet on it. The open book was the crew rosters. Wolflock noticed the Captain's evening shifts had been crossed out starting today and Slavidus was replacing them. Was it because he didn't want to see Himi? Or because he couldn't sleep without Yifi next to him?

The sachet on the desk had candy cane orange and purple stripes with a handwritten card saying:

I know the new can be frightening, but I hope you know we're here for you through your hard time. Always follow your intuition. Smell this bag before sleep or burn it as incense and focus on your destiny for it to become true.

Yours thoughtfully,
B.

Wolflock sniffed the bag and his mind blurred. He gave himself a shake and put the bag down, tugging it open. Within was a sticky array of herbs and a fine purple powder. The purple powder was the same colour as the herb he had collected weeks ago. The other herbs in the bag were the typical potpourri and sweet floral scents often used in incense.

Did the twins bring this herb on board? It was different to what he'd seen earlier. It was processed. Was it a common incense or perfume ingredient? Did they know it made people hazy? Did the haziness make them more open to suggestion?

The threads in his mental web began to combine. He had to stop Slavidus' worries so they could convince him to sail the ship towards the star marking the heart of the mermaid constellation. This meant that he couldn't let Slavidus accept this gift because, if his assumptions about the strange incense were correct, it would make the first mate's anxieties worse. Why was he so afraid of Himi, though? Wolflock had to ask him and find out more.

I should ask Mothy. He's good with people and he'll be able to get the answers we need. I hope he's finished in the kitchen.

His thought was cut short as he saw something large and white flash past Slavidus' window. He thought it was just the kitchen throwing out the dish water, but as a thick dark red droplet slid down the window, Wolflock's blood turned to ice.

"Himi!"

Still gripping the striped bag, he hurtled out of Slavidus' room, down the hall and dodged the people putting up the tent. As fast as his legs could carry him, he raced to the back of the ship. The sight chilled him to his core. A long splash of fresh red liquid ran from the treats Himi hadn't eaten to a short thick harpoon jammed between the deck and railing.

"Himi!" he shouted, gripping the edge of the ship, staring wildly over the edge. The ship was moving so quickly. He couldn't see anything but dark blue water, masking what may be beneath it. "Himi!"

"Wolflock? What happened?" Mothy called from the kitchen window. Wolflock heard him throw whatever he had in his hands down and run for the door.

The scene seared itself into his mind. The exact splatter of the blood, the angle of the harpoon, the three holes in the wood it had been jammed into and ripped free. The leftover treats. Wolflock clutched at his chest, wheezing in agony. He dropped to his knee and yanked the harpoon free.

"Did you lose our notes? The cupboard is open, and I didn't see you come in. Wolflock! What happened?" Mothy repeated, grasping his arm.

Wolflock could only shake his head.

"Is that... blood?!"

"Someone..." Wolflock cried through gritted teeth, "someone hurt Himi and pushed her overboard!"

"That can't be right!"

"Then how do you explain this!?" He stood up and brandished the harpoon. "If you had just watched her while I got the stupid charm, she would have been safe!"

The colour vanished from Mothy's face. "They were right," he whispered, backing away.

"They're charlatans!" Wolflock roared, waving the bloody harpoon in the air. "They've sown anxiety and you've let them get to you instead of using your brain to realise they want something from you!"

"Ever since you fought what they said, everything has gone wrong. Just stop or you're going to get me killed," his whisper trembled as his frightened eyes darted around.

"How could you believe that?"

Mothy pointed at the harpoon, "They said I'd die by harpoon if we stayed friends. I'm sorry, Wolflock, but I-I-I just can't. You have to realise it. You are cursed."

CHAPTER 9

Lost at Sea

Mothy ran.

Wolflock dropped the harpoon, defeated. His mental web had been shredded by a single moment. Or perhaps he had been cursed all along. Perhaps he'd been cursed his whole life. He'd lost his best friend, wasted precious time on getting a ridiculous charm made, and he had let someone kill the creature he owed his life to. He couldn't even solve the case before him.

What was he even doing?

He wasn't cut out to be an investigator. He wasn't even good enough to be on the Guard. He was useless.

The only thing he could do was play a bit of music. Apparently, that had been enough for the goddess of fortune to pigeonhole his entire life into doing just one thing.

No one noticed him slip into the dining hall as they were too enthralled with the tent going up and the discussion around the blessing.

Perhaps he could embrace his fate and say sorry to the sea for being responsible for the death of one of their most unique mermaids. He collected his violin and bow and the bucket of snacks Himi had been so fond of, and, very quietly, made his way to one of the lifeboats. The knots that Grogen had taught him and Mothy a few days ago came in handy, and he managed to lower the boat along the side of the ship without anyone seeing. Not that he cared if they did notice. He could keep them safe by being rude and driving them away. He didn't want anyone else to be harmed because he was cursed.

His thoughts battled savagely as he watched the wake of the ship stream behind them. He had to honour Himi. She had saved his life and then lost hers because of it. He had to find out who harpooned her off the side of the ship. But, at the same time, if he pursued it, he would put everyone in danger.

After an hour or so, he could hear Faleen

demanding everyone sit in particular seats in the tent. He shrank under the shadow of the great metal wing on the port side of the ship as he heard Bleen calling out for him.

"Wolflock! Oh, Wolflock! We're nearly ready for you. I have a piece I want you to play."

Her voice grated on him. He felt like he was just a performing pet to her. Yifi's words about freedom to choose his future rang through his mind, but they just made him feel worse. How could he choose a path that may kill his best friend? Was it even real? Himi had suffered. Of course, it was real. But how could it be so horrid?

"Oh, Mothy dear. You wouldn't have seen Wolflock, have you? He's meant to play for our blessing."

Wolflock looked up at the taffrail to catch a glimpse of Mothy's hair. Had he seen him?

"I don't think Wolflock will want to play. I'm happy to, though. Are we sending the blessing to Parihaan?"

"Mmm.... Thank you, but no. This isn't a blessing as base as those that require drums. And no, again. You're not the quickest ferret in the hole, are you? Silly boy. You don't send blessings to people who don't deserve it. We're blessing the safe journey of the ship to Irid."

He could hear the frown in Mothy's voice. "But we only have two days before Irid. Why would we need to bless the ship's travels? It's done this route for... what? A hundred years?"

"I knew you wouldn't understand. You would be so much better off with your merchant foster father. I hope you head there instead of to the university. I would hate to see you disappointed when they tell you to be cleaning staff. Where is Wolflock?"

"You told me not to be an acquaintance of his anymore. Why would I have seen him?"

"Well," Bleen giggled, "I have seen you both together since then, so I thought you had paid our clear warning no heed."

"I think Wolflock would say that's very presumptuous of you."

Wolflock had never heard Mothy speak so coldly to anyone.

"You wouldn't understand. You haven't had the same education as Faleen and I. We're qualified to speak about such things."

"Sure, you are."

"Well, if you do see him, tell him we're not going

to wait much longer, and he'll miss his mystical debut."

"I'm sure he'll never recover."

Bleen left without another word. Wolflock saw Mothy lean back on the railing for a few moments before he walked away. With a sigh, Wolflock threw one of the dried snacks into the water. Then another. Then another. A long time passed, and he ran out of jerky. The blessing went on for just as long with Faleen giving a drawn out, uncomfortable sermon. He couldn't stand the sound of her high and mighty voice, so he drew out the violin and began to play softly. He just wanted to fill his ears with something pleasant. After a few slow, sad songs, something smacked him on the top of the head. A raw fish fell into the lifeboat and he looked up again. Mothy's elbows poked out over the edge of the ship.

Wolflock's heart lightened. Perhaps if he pursued music, they could still be friends. Or not. Mothy stepped away again. With tired arms, Wolflock put the violin and bow down. Maybe he could summon a good omen again with music, but science would say a fish would do better. He found the small tackle box in the back compartment of the lifeboat and hooked the dead fish to it. Then he had what felt like a stroke of genius. The vibrations of his music may travel down the line and into the water to bring the dolphins faster.

He tied the line to the end of the bow and played. Slowly and lightly to maintain his endurance. If Mothy saw that Wolflock could bring the dolphins with music, then maybe he'd be able to convince him that he had given up investigating.

As the sun set and the sea glittered with peachy light, he could have sworn he saw fins rising and falling out of the water to his right. But no one saw. He couldn't even be sure himself.

He pulled the bait out of the water and saw it had been eaten except for the head. Wolflock shouted to the sea and hurled the violin into the water. His stupid hobby had destroyed his friends, his freedom, his dreams, and lead to the murder of an innocent mermaid. He wanted nothing else to do with music ever.

Wolflock opened his cabin window from outside and crawled through. He got to his waist and his shoe caught something. He struggled for a moment, but his shoe was well and truly stuck. He tried to pull it free once more, but the whole thing came off his foot and he fell with a hard thump into his room.

"This day can't get any worse," he groaned, scrambling to look out his window, but there was no sign of what the shoe was caught on or even of it bobbing away in the distance.

He changed into his pyjamas and tried to write to Myna, but he ended up just scribbling nonsense on the page until he was so tired, he fell asleep at his desk.

In his dreams he saw creatures swimming through the stars. Then they were made of stars. Dolphins, sharks, octopuses. Two old fishing poles with a yellow stain clattered to the ground as he swam towards them. The yellow seeped like incense smoke and turned into an oppressive purple that wrapped around his neck, pulling him away. Wolflock struggled against the smoke, clinging to the threads of a web as the crashing waves buffeted him back and forth. He drew out his magnifying glass and it glowed like fire, dispersing the smoke, and calming the waves.

He could feel himself slipping into a lucid dream, controlling his own actions. The web was filled with loose strands, missing threads and pieces that didn't belong. He had been so focused on finding Sinalta that he hadn't realised there were three layers before him.

The first layer was clear. He could see each thread as aqua, and it smelled like old books. How to find Sinalta. The Captain's old books, the dining hall decorations, dolphins, sharks, octopus.

The second layer of yellow wisps like blood in water and smelling of rotten fish, was who harpooned

Himi overboard and why. The red blood splatter, the harpoon, the stolen notes. The notes came from a cupboard only Wolflock had a key to. He patted himself down and couldn't find it.

"I'll check when I wake. It may be in my breast pocket where I left it."

Then his final layer of silver threads with no scent was why Slavidus didn't like mermaids. The glittering strands included two fishing rods with a yellow-orange stain, his behaviour around Himi and fear of getting close to her, and his urgency to have her removed from the ship.

As if something was telling him he was wrong somewhere, he felt a splash of water in his face. He was still holding the glowing magnifying glass out against the forces that sought to stop him, so it wasn't that. It was a genuine correction, but from where?

A deep, resounding note sang out through the starry blackness and another splash hit him.

"Enough! If this isn't right, tell me what is?"

The echoing beautiful tone turned into a sudden incoherent screech from someone murdering a violin. It only stopped to splash Wolflock in the face again. This time enough water got up his nose to startle him awake. He coughed and spluttered, looking about wildly for the source of the attempted drowning. Then another poorly played string of screeches clawed its way through his door.

Wolflock stood up and threw open his window, leaning so far through he nearly fell out. A smile split across his face when he saw the round white figure of Himi playing the violin as if she were a caricature of a concert player.

"Himi! Himi, you're alive!" he gasped, squirming out of the window, and almost missing the lifeboat as he dropped. She caught his arm and hoisted him into the boat, all the while making purring and snorting noises in her excitement. He threw his arms around her shoulders and pulled her into a tight hug. At first, she froze in shock, but, after a moment, she patted his back as she reached to braid his hair. He took the violin from her and played a quick jovial little tune, making her clap with enthusiasm.

"We have to tell Mothy!" Wolflock scrambled to the other end of the lifeboat and wrenched the window open. "Mothy! Mothy wake up! Himi is alive!"

His friend was sound asleep in his bed and snored loudly in response.

"Mothy!" Wolflock hissed, looking around for something longer than his bow to poke him with.

As he turned back, Himi scooped a handful of

water from the side of the boat and sang a long, low note into it. It froze instantly in the palm of her hand and she passed the chunk of blue ice to Wolflock, understanding what he was trying to do.

As she pressed the ice into his hand, another sense of cold froze him. It felt like the chilling waters he'd fallen into just days ago. Like when he'd found the harpoon with blood. He hesitated. Mothy had said he didn't want to associate with Wolflock anymore. He'd run from the danger. He'd believed opinionated advice so quickly. His best friend had possibly impeded his investigation to save Himi's life and yet...

He didn't want to do this without him. Mothy was his best friend. He nodded to her and flicked the ice at Mothy. It landed right in his ear and he threw his arms and legs out in the dim light as if he were being attacked by bees.

"Mothy! Himi is here! Come quickly!"

It took a few moments for Mothy to understand what was being said, but he slipped out of his window and hugged Himi with just as much enthusiasm. She purred and barked in response, but, as Mothy drew away, his nightshirt caught on something and she yelped.

"What's wrong?" Wolflock frowned, rushing forward, and making the boat swing.

"She's been caught on a hook. Here. Distract her for a second."

Wolflock grabbed his violin and played a little too loudly as Mothy extracted the hook and bit the line to free it.

"See? Nothing to worry about. How did that happen?"

"I... I was trying to bring dolphins to the ship with the fish you kicked down earlier. I put it on a hook and Himi must have found it."

"Don't look so grim. It was no worse than a splinter. She barely bled at all. Yellow blood is a bit new though."

"Yellow blood?" Wolflock saw the yellow-orange blood wiped on her fur in the light shining from the top deck. That meant that Himi hadn't been injured by the harpoon. It had been used for something else when she had fallen.

It also meant that someone had wanted to make it look like she had been killed, but they'd never seen mermaid blood before.

He looked up. Mothy's pleased face upset him. He hadn't wanted to be there solving the case with Wolflock because of what the twins said. Why was he getting enjoyment out of it now?

"I'm so glad she's alive, but I... I don't think we can get her home." As he sighed, he felt crestfallen, slumping forward on his seat.

Mothy sat next to Wolflock on his seat. "What do you mean?"

"I tried really hard, Mothy, but I just couldn't narrow down the location of Sinalta. I'm out of time. And, on top of that," he gestured to the cloudy sky, "there's no way I can see the stars to even try and convince someone to help me navigate. Let alone that someone be Slavidus. The twins were right. I'm just not meant to be an investigator." He held back from saying the word 'we', as it left a bitter taste in his mouth. Mothy had chosen to not help. But he'd been afraid. Wolflock could understand at least that. "I couldn't keep Himi safe. You didn't think I could keep you safe, either. How can I find her home and make sure that stupid prophecy doesn't come true for you, too?"

Mothy bit his lip, frowning. He moved his hand to reach out, but took it back, sighing as he slumped forward in the same position Wolflock was in. "I'm sorry."

"What for?" He turned to look at his friend. "I'm the one who can't get her home. I'm the one she saved the life of."

"For... for not putting my all in. I hid in the kitchen;

I didn't research as much as I could have, and I deserted you when I got frightened. They told me that the closer I got to you, the closer that would bring me to death. I looked at how far we've come and how close I was to Mystentine University and I didn't want to risk it."

A bittersweet sensation ached through him. He wanted to just go back to being great friends, but how could he trust Mothy not to leave him again in the future?

He had to do what others around him were too afraid to do. He had to risk it. Wolflock nudged his elbow with a tiny smile. "I'm sorry I frightened you."

"They said I would never find a home while I stayed with you."

Wolflock started, turning to face Mothy straight on. "That's despicable! How dare they? What rubbish! If it's important to you, you can find a home whenever and wherever you like. I feel like they're just spinning us in circles around each other, relying on us not discussing their terrible manipulations!"

"What did they tell you?" Mothy looked back, hope twinkling in his eyes.

"They told me I would lose everything if I continued investigating. That I was proud, arrogant, not strong enough to overcome some terrible tyrant. That anyone who walked along my path with me would be fraught with dangers. And that, unless I became a musician, I would hurt the people I love."

Mothy gripped his arm so tightly it hurt. "Don't you dare listen to them."

Wolflock and Himi both looked at one another with a quick glance, surprised by his sharp anger.

"Every single person who has ever met you knows you are destined to follow your own path, and they hate it. They're jealous and they're terrified. Anyone who would dissuade you is frightened of you or frightened for you. You are one of the boldest, most determined people I have ever met, and I will..." he lost his words for a moment, "I will be truly unkind to anyone who ever says anything like that to you again."

"Truly unkind is very severe for you, my friend."

Mothy released his arm and nudged his elbow. "I wondered why you were looking so confused and grey after your reading."

"I was just so worried it was the wrong path."

"Who cares if it is? It's the path you chose. Even if you don't walk along it forever, you'll gain so much more by having not been afraid to do it in the first place. Other people's opinions don't reflect the truth of your life. Of your dreams. People shouldn't tell you that it can't be done when you're already doing it."

"Do you always become wise after we have a disagreement?" Wolflock snorted.

"What can I say? Your absence makes me feel cleverer."

"More clever."

"Cleverer-rerer!"

They chuckled for a moment, relieved to be coming back to normal, but still overshadowed by the day's emotional upheavals.

Himi looked back and forth between them with her big pink eyes, flopping her tail into the water and singing to it until it became blue ice, then letting it splash back down and float away.

"Yifi said when we have our fortunes told we have three choices. Fight it, accept it, or prepare for it. What are you going to do?"

"Being on this ship has felt no less like home than when I lived in a travelling caravan. I know I can make my home wherever I go. And, right now, I'm going to Mystentine... with you."

"And the danger?"

"I am fully prepared to stay well away from harpoons. How many can there be in an inland city? I also trust that you'll look after me if I get hurt. I am certain I've already lived through things a hundred times worse than anything you can attract. My home used to be... well... not home."

Wolflock didn't know if it was appropriate to laugh at the terrible joke, but he was saved when Himi brought up two cupped hands of water and sang them into crystal blue ice. She turned it upside down, so it looked like a spire.

"Hrrruum," her voice sounded like bubbles. "Huurummgeh hrruum."

"Himi's.... home?"

Wolflock jaw dropped.

"Mothy! Mothy, that's it!"

"What is?"

"Sinalta isn't a city! It's not an island. It's a glacier! Himi's home is a blue glacier!"

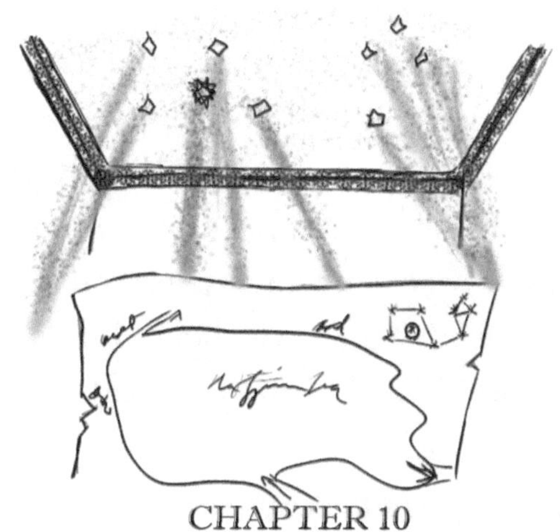

CHAPTER 10

Lift a Curse, Save a
Mermaid

I... don't follow."

"Glaciers float! That's what we learned in our research, which means they drift with the currents, but the currents of the Hatfjorn Sea move in a nine-year pattern due to the volcanic activity under the water. That's why it corresponds with the revealing of the ninth star in the mermaid constellation."

"Yes?" Mothy said slowly as Himi wriggled forward and began braiding his hair.

"That explains why is hasn't been charted on a map. Just like we found when they tried to chart the currents, they couldn't account for the movements. Himi has just shown us she can sing water into blue ice and Sinalta is always described as being crystal blue!"

"But Lockie," Mothy pushed Himi's hands away and started to braid her hair in return, "star or not, how are we going to navigate with a cloudy sky?"

Wolflock frowned. They didn't have time to learn how to navigate alone. He would need help. The only crew working this evening were Slavidus, Kolor, Matroos and Umkombe unless an emergency arose. He didn't want any more crew on deck, as more eyes would mean his plan was under greater scrutiny. At most, they only had eight hours until dawn.

His thoughts drifted to the present Bleen had left for Slavidus. The mind-numbing incense. What if it could be used for a good purpose?

His gut twisted at the idea of using it on Slavidus when it had made him more anxious. There was so much at stake if Slavidus didn't change his mind.

"I have a terrible idea," Wolflock sighed.

"Normally I'd laugh and be on board, but this looks serious. What are you thinking?"

"The twins left Slavidus a sachet of the incense

they've been using in their readings. It has a herb in it that is purple and creates a suggestable, hazy fog through the mind. We need to help Slavidus understand that Himi is not a danger to him and that if he helps us, he'll be better off."

"I don't like that."

"I don't either. I want to have it as a second plan. I think I know enough about why he's frightened of mermaids to speak with him. I just need you to be ready to use it if I give the signal."

Mothy nodded, looking from Himi to the ship. "I'll help. What's the plan?"

They devised the plan, step by step. Firstly, they had to get Himi into the dining hall. As the only enclosed public space, it would serve as the best place to use the incense if needed. Secondly, they had to lure Slavidus into the dining hall where Wolflock could use the clues he'd found to confront Slavidus' fears. The third step was to get him to help sail them to Sinalta.

Wolflock neglected to tell Mothy that any location around the mermaid's heart would put them almost a day and a half from their next port destination. He was prepared to take all the punishment for their deviancy, so, the less Mothy knew, the less trouble he'd be in.

Mothy hoisted the lifeboat high enough for him

and Himi to peek onto the deck, while Wolflock climbed back through his porthole window to collect the bag of incense. He made his way to the open deck, feeling his heart quicken as he was faced with the open space at night on agitated waters. He could see Slavidus looking ahead with little concern for what else was happening on the deck.

Wolflock waved for Mothy and Himi to move to the dining hall. They slipped onto the grey wood deck and started moving in the shadows. They were feet from the door when Himi barked, bouncing to something on the ground she put in her mouth. One of the dried snacks!

"Huh?" Slavidus turned his head towards them.

"Slavidus!" Wolflock shouted. He didn't think they'd need a distraction but, apparently, he was it. "I have something I need to ask you."

"And what would that be, Mr Felen?"

Mothy rolled Himi to the dining hall as Wolflock reached the base of the helm stairs. "I want to know..." he paused. How was he going to approach this? Did he want to make Slavidus mad? Appeal to his compassion? Spark his curiosity? How was he to do any of that?

Himi 'arf'ed as she saw heard Wolflock, making Slavidus look around suspiciously.

"Why did you harpoon Himi?" he shouted as a crackle of thunder rippled overhead.

"What?"

"I know you didn't want her on the ship. Why didn't you just keep away from her? Why did you have to kill her?"

"I did nothing of the sort! I haven't touched the creature since she came on board!" Slavidus looped a cord around a spoke of the wheel to hold it steady. "What is the meaning of these accusations?"

"I know you did it and I can prove it! You hated her and I want to know why!"

"You are playing a dangerous game, Mr Felen. What has come over you? Did the creature bewitch you?" the first mate took a few steps towards Wolflock.

"You're going to have to answer to the captain! I'm going to tell him everything!"

Slavidus' face paled and he stepped closer again, but Wolflock stepped back. There it was. The moment where the energy sparked into the beginning of a chase. Slavidus didn't know what was happening, but he wasn't going to risk losing his livelihood on false accusations. His honour wouldn't allow it. Wolflock was well aware of this.

With the hint of a smirk, he took off towards the

cabins. Slavidus pushed off from the stairs, running after him. Just before he got to the stairs, Wolflock took a hard right, circled around the centre mast, and threw himself into the dining hall.

Slavidus ran in after him and stopped. Wolflock couldn't help it. He had slid into one of the dining chairs and as Slavidus had come in after him, he'd posed as if he'd been there all along. Matroos, who was on evening cook duties stopped wiping the dishes stopped and stared, waiting for what was to happen next.

"Take a seat, my good man and let's talk."

Slavidus' chest rose and fell with exertion and he looked around as if he were waiting for others to jump out and say it was a joke.

"What... What on Pelaia are you doing?"

"Helping solve a mystery," he smiled and gestured across the table to him.

Slavidus rubbed his forehead and after a moment, he obliged. "I did not hurt that mermaid."

"Oh, I know that. Well, you didn't hurt Himi. I just needed to get you to a place we could speak freely. Matroos, can we get a bottle of cordial?"

"You know where it is, Wolflock." The cook rolled his eyes.

"Good man." Wolflock dismissed him. "Now," he

put the tips of his fingers together, "tell me about your first two mermaids."

"I don't know what you're talking about."

"Oh? Well, your fishing poles would say otherwise. You know I only recently found out that mermaids have an odd yellowy-orange blood. I suppose you didn't want to touch the rods ever again, which is why they didn't get cleaned for all these years, but you can't part with them as they're a constant reminder that if you hurt one more mermaid you'll be cursed to drown, correct? But my question is: Did you kill the first two or just injure them?"

Slavidus' face dropped and he sighed. "I made this one easy for you, didn't I?"

"On the contrary. This has been a mess of a mystery until recently. I knew you didn't like Himi, but it was more than that. You were frightened of being anywhere near her. That's how I knew, when I found your harpoon on the deck, that it wasn't you who had done it. And, when I saw red liquid, I presumed it was her blood. Then I was enlightened by Mothy that mermaids don't bleed red blood."

Slavidus nodded and took a deep breath in. "I have killed one mermaid and injured a second. The first became tangled in my fishing line when I was fishing for sharks. He banged so hard into the side of the ship that he never woke up. The second... I don't know. I was fishing and my hook got caught as the ship moved. I pulled it up to see the mermaid, but the hook pulled free and all I saw were plumes of yellow blood. I've never fished since."

"You believe a third instance will curse you."

"No. I know it will. I love the water so much. I'm born under the mermaid sign. I dishonour my very stars by my actions. I could bring a terrible fate onto the ship and crew I love so much." His stormy eyes filled with tears and he put his face in his hands. "Why am I cursed to hurt the things I love so much?"

Wolflock let the moment wash over them before he spoke again. "What if you could heal the damage you've done? What if you can restore justice and harmony to your stars?"

"How can I? May fate has been foretold."

A flash of lightning filled the windows of the dining hall and Wolflock's mind.

"And now that you know your future, you have three choices."

The first mate looked up with a confused frown.

"You can accept it, fight it, or prepare for it. Your future is fluid, and it is always up to you until it comes to pass. Why would you choose to live in fear when you can make a difference?"

"What are you talking about? You said it yourself, lad. She's gone. Even if she were still here, we could never take her home. No one has ever found Sinalta."

Wolflock grinned and glanced back where he thought Mothy and Himi were hiding. Nothing.

"Uh... Give me a second."

He felt bad leaving Slavidus there alone and confused, but the theatrics of his reveal had been disappointed as well. He dashed from the dining hall and to the centre mast where Mothy was scratching his head.

"Where is Himi? Why did you leave?"

"You two were in such a good discussion and Himi growled at the incense bag, so I brought her out here and then I blinked and now she's gone!"

"Gone?"

They heard a chair tip over in the dining hall and Slavidus shouted.

"Himi!"

They ran to the hall and threw open the doors. The sight before them made both their jaws drop. Slavidus had knocked his chair over when he stood up, surprised to see Himi coming through the door. She dragged her white body towards him, bobbing high up as she moved. Slavidus stood frozen in place, only twitching when she started to hum. A long, deep tone came from her chest as she approached him. She tilted her head, watching his hand reach out to her.

"I... I'm so sorry. Please forgive me."

"Wolflock, look!" Mothy tugged at his sleeve, pointing to the gemstones in the wall.

Slavidus' hand stopped inches before he touched Himi's face. She took his hand with her webbed fingers and placed it on her hair, opening her mouth to sing.

Slavidus burst into tears, kneeling before her, and the gemstones in the dining hall glowed brightly.

"Get the lamps!" Wolflock whispered hurriedly, running to take down the lights around the room.

They covered them with a tablecloth, sinking the room into darkness. Rays of light emanated from the blue gemstones, bouncing off the mirrors and projecting around the room like ripples in the sea. Wolflock, Mothy, Matroos and Slavidus looked up as Himi continued singing. The gemstone set in the compass was the brightest light, pointing at the constellation's heart.

"That's it!" Wolflock cried out, "That's Sinalta! Slavidus! That's where we need to go!"

Himi finished her song and Mothy removed the tablecloth from the lanterns as the room darkened again.

Slavidus' head was bowed, and he didn't look up for a long moment. He held her hand as he brought himself to his feet and looked up at the ceiling, drawing in one more deep breath.

"If you think for a moment, I can get us to Sinalta alone in the middle of the night, you have vastly overestimated my capabilities."

Wolflock's heart sank. "But-"

"You'd better be able to tie a better knot, Mr Felen. If we're getting her home without the Captain stopping us, you and Mr Enitnelav better be ready to work until you bleed."

CHAPTER 11
Sinalta Ahoy!

"Uh..."

"Oh yes, sir. You're about to have a hard lesson on how a ship runs."

"But-"

"If you haven't had a good enough sleep, tough luck. If you want to get to her home before the Captain changes our course, hop to! Matroos, we have a heading. Mothy is your apprentice. Wolflock, Kolor will tell you what to do."

He charged out of the dining hall, followed by Himi. Matroos grabbed Mothy and Wolflock's collars and hauled them out after him.

"Unfurl the sails! Kolor! Wolflock is your help. Full speed ahead and hold on tight!"

Kolor grinned, bearing her sharp canines as she helped pull Wolflock up the forward rigging. Every sail pillowed with the wind pushing them forward. The storm held its breath, leaving them dry as the lightning flashed along the waves they had to surmount. Adrenaline ran through his veins as he tried to follow Kolor's instructions while holding on for dear life. He could have sworn the waves grew higher and higher whenever he had to let go of the mast. He held lines back, tied them off and loosed them on command, racing around as the weather and direction changed.

While they were on the deck Himi chased them back and forth, checking their handiwork by chewing on it. After several hours, Wolflock began to drag his feet. Sleep felt like a weighted coat around his shoulders. As he changed one of the knots for the sails, he saw Himi race past him to the bow. He reached out, thinking she would leap off, but she stopped when she reached the railing.

Himi lifted her head high, sniffing the air. The sea began to relax, smoothing out as a sleepy fog shrouded them. Wolflock made his way to the helm and sat on the stairs, keeping an eye on Himi. Mothy spotted him sitting and slumped over, lying face down on the stairs.

"We should be there by dawn," Slavidus nodded. "Good work, lads."

"Do you think you'll get in trouble, Slavidus?" Mothy mumbled into the stairs.

"Oh, probably. It's worth it though. We've done a good thing."

Wolflock stopped staring at Himi's shining white hair to reach his hand out to Slavidus.

"Give me your compass."

"What?"

"I never intended for anyone but me to get into any trouble. Give me your compass and we'll tell the captain I broke it, so your navigation was impaired."

"That... that's actually very kind of you. And clever. I can't let you do that though."

"Yes, you can. Pass it to me."

"Do it, Slavidus. He's too stubborn. Can't beat him," Mothy mumbled.

The first mate rolled his eyes and handed over his compass for Wolflock to fiddle with. As they sailed over the glassy waters, a reverential silence fell over them. Himi started to sing into the fog, her resonating tones bringing an ethereal magic to the ship. Wolflock thought he heard it echo back, but his mind jolted awake.

"Mermaids!" he whispered.

The golden sun melted the fog as it split the horizon. He stood up and moved to Himi's side as she sang, but the echo didn't return. Wolflock wondered if they were still on the right track. The glacier moved, so it may not be directly under the star. He had to help. He turned back and collected his violin from the lifeboat, and re-joined Himi, playing along with her song.

Wolflock lost himself in the song he'd composed for Himi, adding the long deep tones she had sung. The moment felt perfect. The anticipation of finding the solution to the mystery brought him a sense of completion. Mothy found his drum in the dining hall, and started a slow heartbeat rhythm. The three of them brought their music to the front of the ship in a beautiful moment of connectedness.

Wolflock began to realise that music was indeed a part of him. It brought him clarity, but it wasn't all of him. He loved music. The patterns, the freedom, the constraint. The pure creation. But it was only part of him. His heart had to find answers as much as his mind did.

Chunks of blue ice began floating past the ship, making dull thunking noises as they bumped into the hull. Wolflock finished his song, giving his arm a short rest, but, as he lifted it to begin again, Himi stopped singing and they heard the echo again.

They looked out, seeing a misty dark shape coming closer along the horizon.

"Is that...?"

"Sinalta ahoy!" Slavidus shouted, "Kolor! Ring the bell! Sinalta ahoy!"

The Silver Ice Hair sailed through the blue ice, bringing the towering frozen spires into view as dark figures swam around the ship. The water splashed, making Himi shift back and forth as if she was sizing up whether to jump.

"Come on, Himi. Let's get you home."

"Drop anchor," Slavidus called out as he saw them move to the lifeboat and fastened the wheel to meet them there. He smiled from his heart as he touched her shoulder in farewell.

"Thank you."

"Hrrrruum," she purred before following Wolflock into the lifeboat.

"I'll lower you both down."

"Goodbye, Himi! Thank you for saving Lockie. I won't let him fall out of the boat anymore," Mothy waved, drumming enthusiastically.

They lowered Wolflock and Himi down, letting

the lifeboat settle in the water. Himi sang out across the water. Dark figures swam under the ship back and forth, glimpsing up at them, the echo of their song coming back. Wolflock played his violin to draw them up, and, after a few minutes, a pair of webbed hands the size of frying pans gripped the side of the boat.

A black-haired head peeked over the top with two jet black eyes, blinking as they looked around the lifeboat. The mermaid was so huge that a touch of trepidation caught in Wolflock throat. He just hoped they didn't tip the boat.

Himi made a high pitched trill and launched herself off the edge of the boat, rocking it dangerously. The pair disappeared into the water and Wolflock smiled. It didn't feel like much of a goodbye, but she was safe and that was all he wanted. He took a moment to play the song he'd made her for and felt a sense of bittersweet melancholy hold him.

Wolflock took a deep sigh and stood up, ready to be raised back up, when the whole boat tipped to the side. He looked over to see Himi pulling half of her body onto the boat.

"Himi! You came back!" He dropped the violin to hug her around the shoulders.

She hugged him back, purring against his shoulder.

"Urfurf." She pushed him back and slipped back into the water so just her shoulders were out. She reached out with something in her hand.

With a raised eyebrow he held his palm out for her and she dropped a peach sized blue gemstone into his palm. At its centre was an air bubble filled with a small pocket of water.

"Hrruum," she said in her bubbly voice.

"Home," Wolflock nodded.

"Gehbuh, Urfurf."

And she slipped back into the water. Wolflock watched as her shining white form vanished into the depths.

"Goodbye, Himi."

196

CHAPTER 12

Fortunes Returned

Mothy hoisted Wolflock back up to the deck and smiled at him with pure exhaustion in his face.

"We did it."

"We did it."

"You're blessed, my friend."

Wolflock rolled his eyes and put his arm around Mothy's shoulders as they made their way to the cabins. "I will probably have to fight against that, too."

"She blessed you. I wouldn't worry about it being too troublesome."

Many of the passengers had been woken by the

bell and were in awe of the creatures around them. As the boys reached the entrance to the stairs a great purple and orange mass blocked their way.

"How wonderful it is that you used your music to find this place!" Bleen simpered. "It is so magical! So-"

"Unlikely," Faleen cut her off. "I hope you realised that every time you fought the music you failed and that your success came from song."

Wolflock raised a tired eyebrow at her. "Mothy, you go on to sleep. I'll speak to you later."

"Are you sure?"

"Unequivocally."

Mothy shrugged and scooted past them.

"I've been thinking about what you both said to me and many of the other people on board. It has done what may be irreparable damage to the happiness and mental foundations of all on board. And for what? A power fantasy?" He looked at Bleen, who flushed crimson.

"T-they just don't understand it, yet! It's for their own good!"

"No. No, it's not. It's for your own agenda. You have put each and every person here into a tight little box and cut the edges off that don't suit your impression of what they should be. You were put in a position of authority and you abused it. But tell me, did you know your sister tried to fake the murder of a mermaid and drugged everyone on board with a psychoactive herb I've experienced before?"

"What?" Bleen gasped, going pale and looking to her sister, whose nose had curled into a snarl.

"I can only assume the poorly thought-out sabotage to our investigation was your doing, Bleen, under the urging of your sister. Stealing our notes from the cupboard when you took the key after pawing my clothes earlier and telling Slavidus to believe the information about a curse on himself. Juvenile, really, but harder to track than the faked murder of Himi."

"You are talking nonsense because you're upset with us telling you the truth about your foolish career choice," Faleen sniffed, rolling her eyes.

"Oh, am I? If you hadn't exerted yourselves on some weird illusion that you could control others where you had to make everyone on board miserably abide by your fortunes, I might have even considered what you said. But your cold mannerisms, the sheer rudeness to my friend, and the cruelty with which you have displayed have well and truly dispelled the notion of you being competent or well-travelled."

Wolflock wished he had more of an audience, but, as the crew and company were enthralled by the mermaids, he felt he would have to be satisfied with standing two stairs taller than the twins.

"You couldn't get the harpoon in the wood deep enough to leverage Himi off the ship, could you? That's why you had to try three times before you found the right crook to wedge it into? I saw the marks. Also, I think someone better travelled would know that mermaids don't bleed red blood like the ointment you had in your basket. They bleed yellow. They'd also know that only cheap teas are preserved with sulphur."

"You have no proof." Faleen's eyes were wide.

"Oh? Well, I'm certain I can show the captain and Slavidus the same staining residue from the ointment on the harpoon and on the pristine grey wood you've tarnished. I can also give them a clear example of how you poisoned everyone on board with this." He threw the orange and purple striped bag into the air.

Faleen's face devolved into pure fury. "What is *that*?"

Bleen shrank. "Slavidus was so upset... I put it together to help him stay to his destiny."

"Yes. It's a perfect sample of your mind-numbing incense. Tell me, did you test it in the tuiti fruit stew a few weeks ago as well?"

Both of them looked confused, making Wolflock

sigh.

"No matter. You're going to give everyone a fresh reading out in this beautiful sea air. I'm going to watch and listen. You're going to fix the damage you've done. And, if you don't, I'm taking all of this to the captain, at which point you'll be arrested and sent to the nearest Guard Tower for much harder labour than a repeat of your terrible services. Understand?"

Faleen screamed at him through clenched teeth and Bleen chased after her back into their cabin.

"Wolflock? What have you done now?" Captain Blutro yawned as he approached Wolflock from the dining hall, catching a glimpse of the twins' response to him.

"Oh! I didn't know you were awake. Nothing too out of the ordinary, sir."

"No. That is the problem. My office, lad. We have a few things to discuss."

"But Captain, I'm exhausted. Can't I sleep first?"

"Not a chance on Pelaia. Move along."

Wolflock's muscles ached all over and his hands felt blistered from the work he'd done all night. He followed the Captain into his study, flopping into the chair across from him.

"Now... What am I to make of this?"

"Uhh..." he thought hard for a moment, making sure he didn't incriminate Mothy or Slavidus. "I felt I owed a debt to Himi, the mermaid, for saving my life the other night, so I was determined to get her home."

"I understand that part. What I don't understand is how we went from arriving in Irid today, to now being a full day and a half behind?"

"Ah... well... I tampered with Slavidus' compass after I determined the location of Sinalta. As it was a cloudy night, he had to navigate by it."

"And Mothy?"

"Oh, he was just on mermaid watching duty. Didn't know anything at all."

"Hmm... I see. Well, this puts me in an advantageous position."

"Pardon?" Wolflock blinked as he sat up. How was this a good thing for the Captain?

"Oh yes. You have been a significant pest on my vessel, albeit an entertaining one. With these damages, your previous fee has now escalated above the level that was paid and I doubt there is anything you can offer to make amends for this."

"Captain? I don't-"

"You're going to work on my ship until we reach Creast, Mr Felen. You're going to do each and every task set for you in the most efficient manner. You'll not complain, you'll not slack off. You are going to be instrumental in catching up the time we have lost. You'll be starting on the night shift tonight and day shift tomorrow, so go get a good sleep. You'll need it." The captain grinned manically.

Wolflock slouched forward and groaned. "Why do you always have to punish my fun, sir?"

"How else am I meant to keep you out of trouble? If you're going to meddle with my ship, you're going to do it on my terms."

Dixer Meer Felen

Wir habe nicht muns aber I habe ein tag wir kennen.
I bin ein Freund von Wolflod. Meine Menam is Mathy.
Ihr hab nicht fragt mich zu schreib, aber I
denkent de etwas kennt wes hab nur geseknet
veruract Ihr is nicht abentet zu mitteilen dazuen.
I habe schreib lahtere zu mich famale und I
denkent es yes seltsamer fumf Wolflod zu nicht
schreib.

Ihr hab nur ein toll Freund und I habe dennach muns
dazuen mehr entschlossen zu habe er teo. Fur dess
letzte woch Ihr errette der leben von ein wess
Meerjungfrau und fonds ein ress blau Glavca hat
des der mythenhaft stadt von Sinalta. I annehmen es
is nicht mythenhaft dazumer ernct Ihr entsecht es.

Ich von der uroach I bin schreibet is dat vorher
dis. Wolflod was nicht gefuhl gut und hab einen
ungluck wo Ihr was feerne af der schepp. Es was
durch nicht eine fehler, aber I was haffet zu frag dis
zu schreib zu Ihrm. Ihr hab gefens lahtere urom
Ihrem erroter, aber nicht dis. I kennt es wurde
bedeuten ein rel zu Ihrem und dat der par uroach
Ihr hab nicht schreibe zuror is veruract Ihr is
hartnachis.

I habe dis eind ein tastich gefund und I bitch
vorder zu ein tag treffet dis.

Dinen Jublenet,

Mathy Snitnelay

About the Author

Rhiannon is the walker between worlds. One foot in Earth, the other constantly stepping into Pelaia. As if gazing into a crystal ball, she sees this other world and all that happens within it with the clarity of someone staring through a veil. It is her purpose in life to transcribe these histories, adventures and mysteries for you to enjoy.

This witchy woman was raised by a fairy who taught her that there are all kinds of magic throughout the world. She taught Rhiannon to withhold judgement because you never truly know another's story. She also taught her that everyone, no matter how flawed, has something to give.

The adventures of Rhiannon's youth lead her through trials and dangers that taught her about the darkness within the world, but it also showed her that anything could be overcome. There was always a way. Surrounded by so much apathy and hopelessness, Rhiannon made it her goal in life to show others the light and that if they could dream it they could do it.

The way she was shown this was through stories.

Stories of friendship, love, adventure, discovery, compassion, understanding, and kindness. All of these stories gave her new friends, new lessons, new life.

In the depths of her darkest place during year 11 and 12, when she felt at her loneliest, drugs surrounded her life in terrible ways, the self worth of those she loved and admired crumbled, she was relentlessly bullied and felt friendless in her most trying years, she lived in squalor due to bureaucratic errors, and yet she still had to be "perfect". She had to perfectly excel in school, she had to perfectly remain calm and gentle in the face of abusive men, she had to be a perfect role model for all those around her. That craving for perfection in order to get love nearly killed her several times. In all of this darkness with politicians sacrificing real people and real environments for imaginary money, with teachers displaying no compassion for their students, with men abusing women and children, with communities vilifying those who needed them most, with injustice reigning and all hope seemingly lost... Puinteyle was born.

All of these pains in life were fixed in Puinteyle.

All of them were able to be mended and healed because of a conscientious effort. The people of Puinteyle wanted to be better than their problems. Puinteyle was where people made an effort to love freely and always sought to help each other, animals and the environment. Harmony. True and beautiful harmony. Where the pendulum never swayed too far away from that beautiful harmonious and happy point of balance.

But like in our lives, there is always obstacles to overcome and darkness to understand. Therefore, Puinteyle would always have its own inner turmoils to learn and grow from too. Thus, the stories never truly end.

Rhiannon has always lived and breathed stories, knowing her role in life is to be this guide through a new world for others. Her dream is to support her community with her stories, as well as creating a company where other artists can come together in celebration of Pelaia and all it has to offer.

Get More of the Magic & Mystery…

subscribe.rhiannoneltonauthor.com/more

If you want more clues, more magic and more mystery, let me know by going to the Case of the Captain's Hair subscribe page.

You'll get clues, maps, sketches, behind the scenes stories, lore and much more! You'll also be the first to know when a new story is coming out so you can solve the mystery before your friends.

If you sign up with the magical link below, you'll also get a free downloadable map to follow Wolflock's journey to Mystentine University.

subscribe.rhiannoneltonauthor.com/more

Thank you for being part of the magic and supporting an independently published Australian author! Australia's independent authors need the support of their local community to continue to produce the books we all love.

If you enjoyed this book, please leave a positive review online (where you purchased the book or on Goodreads), recommend this book to your friends or family, or purchase another copy to gift to a loved one.

Stay tuned for the next mystery in the series:

THE WOLFLOCK CASES

BOOK 7

THE CASE OF THE PISCES MOON

www.rhiannoneltonauthor.com

 RhiDElton

 RhiannonEltonAuthor

 RhiDElton

 rhiannoneltonauthor

 Rhiannon D. Elton

 RhiDElton

THE WOLFLOCK CASES

1. The Case of the Captain's Hair - Now Available

2. The Case of Mothy - Now Available

3. The Case of the Curse of Houl - Now Available

4. The Case of the Bitter Draught – Now Available

5. The Study in Silver - Now Available

6. The Case of the Lost Mermaid - Now Available

7. The Case of the Pisces Moon - May 2021

8. The Case of the Haemophageous Equine - July 2021

9. The Case of the Lost Antrum - September 2021

10. The Case of the Mountain's Monster - December 2021

www.ingramcontent.com/pod-product-compliance
Lightning Source LLC
Chambersburg PA
CBHW030425120726
47903CB00003B/811